Knotted Up In Pink Yarn

A Witch's Cove Mystery
Book 13

Vella Day

Knotted Up In Pink Yarn
Copyright © 2021 by Vella Day
Print Edition
www.velladay.com
velladayauthor@gmail.com

Cover Art by Jaycee DeLorenzo
Edited by Rebecca Cartee and Carol Adcock-Bezzo

Published in the United States of America
Print book ISBN: 978-1-951430-35-1

ALL RIGHTS RESERVED. No part of this book may be used or reproduced in any manner whatsoever without written permission of the author except in the case of brief questions embodied in critical articles or reviews.

This is a work of fiction. Names, characters, places, and incidents either are the product of the author's imagination or are used fictitiously, and any resemblance to actual persons living or dead, business establishments, events or locales, is entirely coincidental.

Witch's Cove might have a rejected gargoyle familiar and a vandalized yarn shop, but even murder can't stop this love story.

As an amateur sleuth, who happens to be a witch, I, Glinda Goodall, eventually get to the bottom of the who-dun-its. But when a gargoyle goes missing from atop a church, I don't know where to begin to look. If that wasn't troublesome enough, a vandal has strung pink yarn across the French inspired yarn shop. Was it kids again? Or someone more nefarious?

My only hope of figuring out this mystery is to join the women's knitting group. I'm such a sucker for gossip. But me, knit? It won't be pretty. Besides, do I really need a sweater in July—in Florida no less?

Anyone willing to send me some tips on knitting, please do. I need all the help I can get on these cases.

Chapter One

MY BEST FRIEND, Penny, rushed into my apartment carrying a bottle of red wine, waving a small bag, the scent of something spicy wafting in front of her. Cookies, perhaps? Or was she trying out a new perfume? She was wearing more make-up than usual. Hmm. Maybe she'd come from visiting her boyfriend.

"You have to see what I made you." She was panting because the stairs up to my place were rather long and steep.

"What did you bring me?" I couldn't remember when Penny had ever made me anything, but I was excited nonetheless. I took the proffered bottle of wine and set it on the scarred, wooden coffee table that would have to be replaced one of these days. "I'll get us some glasses. It seems like forever since we've had a girls' night."

"Tell me about it." She sat down on the sofa and patted the seat cushion next to her, signaling Iggy to join her.

No surprise, my pink iguana rushed over to her. He loved Penny probably because she always told him how smart he was. I quickly retrieved the corkscrew, grabbed two wine glasses that had been through the dishwasher one too many times, and returned to the living room.

I plopped down next to my friend and placed our celebration items on the coffee table. She understood it was her job to open the wine since she was really good at using the corkscrew. Only then did I notice the label on the bottle. It was the wine my grandmother used to drink, and my heart warmed. Nana always had a glass before dinner, claiming it calmed her soul.

But enough reminiscing. I didn't want to tear up, or Penny would think something bad had happened—which it hadn't. Of late, though, I had been missing my grandmother more than ever, probably because she'd come to me in her ghostly form quite a lot lately. I cleared my throat. "Can I open my present now?"

"Absolutely. I just finished it yesterday."

It? Not them, as in a dozen cookies? I wasn't aware that Penny was the arts and crafts type, though she'd surprised me in the past, like when she made her waitressing costume. My aunt, who was the owner of the Tiki Hut Grill, insisted we wear a costume to work. No surprise, Penny had sewn pennies all over her skirt. That made her outfit a bit noisy but cute. It was quite clever and always a hit with the customers. I used to dress up as Glinda the Good Witch, in part because I liked wearing pink, and in part because my name is Glinda. My magic wand that doubled as a pencil could be purchased in the gift store.

Penny might not have changed all that much in the last four years since we became friends, but I had. I was no longer waitressing with her at my aunt's restaurant. Instead, I was now running my own business, the Pink Iguana Sleuths with my boyfriend, Jaxson Harrison—something I swore I never wanted, or rather, would never have. And I'm talking about not wanting or having a boyfriend. I'd always dreamed of running my own business.

As for Jaxson, I'm glad I didn't stick to my rule of being totally independent. He was the best thing to come into my life. Thanks to his influence, as well as my cousin, Rihanna's, I was branching out in the wardrobe department, too. While I always wore my signature pink somewhere, that color no longer dominated my entire look. I was actually wearing blue jeans right now. Okay, I had on pink sneakers, but my white t-shirt should count for something.

I picked up the paper gift bag, opened it, and looked inside. No smell floated upward, so it wasn't cookies. Darn. With the wad of white tissue paper on top of the gift, I couldn't tell what was inside. Since I trusted Penny not to play a joke on me, I stuck my hand in and pulled out a soft, squishy item that I couldn't identify.

"Hmm." I flipped it over, but it looked the same from both sides. It was some sort of knitted pink and green *thing*. It was about four inches wide and maybe eight inches long. "Is it a potholder?"

She laughed as she uncorked the bottle of Merlot. "No, silly. Look at the two loops on one end and the buttons on the other."

That didn't clear up anything. I huffed out a laugh. "Of course, it's a beer cozy." I rarely drank beer, but maybe it was for Jaxson when he came over. Though I'd never seen an eight-inch tall beer can before.

Hmm. The stitches were a little uneven, implying this might have been Penny's first knitting attempt.

She rolled her eyes as she uncorked the wine. "No. Give it

to me. I'll show you."

Once she finished pouring the two glasses, she handed me my drink. Penny then adjusted Iggy on her lap and wrapped the coaster-thingy around his body, buttoning it in place. "It's a sweater for Iggy. You know how cold he gets in the winter."

It was July, but I didn't think it wise to mention that fact. "It fits him perfectly." Or it kind of did. It might even stay on as long as he didn't move too fast. "What do you say, Iggy?"

Iggy wiggled his body and then looked up at Penny. "Thank you. I love it."

And yes, my iguana could talk. I am a witch, after all, and Iggy is my familiar.

Penny grinned. "See? I knew you would. Glinda, you have to come with me to the yarn shop Sunday for our knitting circle. You could make all sorts of things for Iggy."

Oh, joy. "That's okay. I'm not really the knitting type." At least not anymore. That being said, I did love the feel of the soft wool, the brilliant colors, and the soothing clacking of the needles, but who had time for that? Even if Jaxson and I weren't working on a case, if I had some spare time, I'd rather be reading a book.

"Do you think I am the artsy type?"

"Not all the time, so why did you really go there?" Something was going on with her.

"Hello! The gossip."

"We get plenty of gossip from the ladies." My aunt being one of the biggest participants. Okay, Dolly Andrews, the owner of the Spellbound Diner might be the biggest gossip queen in town, though in truth, she learned most of her news from the sheriff's grandmother, Pearl Dillsmith. "Maybe I should ask you who is in this knitting group of yours?"

Penny already had a hunky boyfriend, so it wasn't as if she was looking to find someone—not that I'd expect many men to show up, but you never know.

"I've only been twice, and both times, different women have been there. Have you met the new owner yet?"

Was she avoiding answering my question for a reason? "No. I've yet to stop in the new store." It was aptly named, *Fifi's Yarns*. Clearly, I needed to go sooner rather than later. I loved mysteries. I raised my glass. "I heard she's French."

Penny shook her head and then sipped her wine. "She just likes people to think that. While I could detect a bit of an accent, I think it might be fake. The shop is covered in French artifacts, though. She has a three foot tall replica of the Eiffel Tower, baskets full of plastic baguettes, a pile of empty wine bottles next to plates of fake cheese, and some random statues. One is Rodin's Thinker. It makes sense, I guess, since her name is Fifi LaRue." Penny rolled her eyes.

I knew her name, but that was all. "I have no room to talk about funny names." In case it wasn't obvious, I was named after the good witch in *The Wizard of Oz*. "Fifi LaRue does seem a little made up to me."

"Right? Fifi is better suited for a dog than a person."

I chuckled and then sipped my wine. Oh, yum. The smooth oak flavor slid down my throat. Go Nana. She had good taste in wine, and now apparently so did Penny. "Exactly. I would have thought Lulu, Cheri, Angelique, or even Juliette would be better suited as a name. They scream authentic French names, just as much if not more so, than Fifi."

"Totally."

"You said you didn't get the sense she was on the up and up." Penny nodded. "I'll ask Jaxson to do a little digging on her. Was it because her accent sounded fake? Or was it more than that?"

Penny was my human lie detector. Being a witch, she had talents above and beyond others. It was just a shame that she didn't work on polishing her magical skills—like I should be doing.

"I can't say exactly."

"Did she say why she decided to settle in Witch's Cove and use a fake name—assuming it is fake?"

"It may be real. Her name could be Félice, and she is just going by Fifi."

"You're probably right. Everyone should be allowed to be whomever they want to be."

"Regardless, I sensed something was off, which was why I want to keep attending the knitting circle. She's different, I'll tell you that." Penny sipped her wine, and then closed her eyes for a moment, clearly enjoying the full-bodied flavor.

"Different how?" I asked.

She pressed her lips together. "I can't quite put my finger on it, but she seems angry and a bit ill at ease around people."

"Most shop owners are very outgoing. What do you know about her, other than she seems to love knitting and France?"

"She's likes to talk, which is probably why she started the knitting circle."

"Liking to talk and being ill at ease around people don't seem to go together."

"I should have said, she'll chat about what she wants to

talk about. I don't get the sense she is a good listener."

That could be said about a lot of people. Iggy pawed at the sweater, probably because he was overheating. "Come here, Iggy. We don't want to ruin the sweater before winter."

"Yeah. I don't want to get it dirty." If he could roll his eyes, he would be doing just that.

I removed his wrapper—a name that seemed more appropriate than sweater since the yarn didn't cover his legs. "I don't know why I haven't stopped over at the shop yet and welcomed her to Witch's Cove, but we were kind of busy trying to correct something that went wrong in the past at the candy store." Like a dead body being stuffed in the wall.

"You mean your trip to Ohio?"

"Yup." That had been another night of popcorn, wine, and much candy to get through that story. "So, what else can you tell me about this Fifi woman."

"She's very put together in a French aristocratic sort of way. I'd say she's probably in her late thirties and is very pretty. Here's the thing: She seems both angry and unhappy. I think it could be because she was recently divorced."

"That would make anyone upset or depressed. Do we know where she is from?"

"Somewhere near the Florida Panhandle, I think, but I can't be sure. I was concentrating on trying to make my stitches even that I didn't catch all of the facts. If you look closely, you'll see I wasn't all that successful at keeping things in a straight line."

"It's the thought that counts. It is sweet of you to think of my familiar."

"I swear some of the women don't even need to look at

what they are doing, and their rows come out perfect."

It was as if she hadn't heard a word I'd said. "I'm sure it's a matter of practice. What are you working on next?"

"A cap for Tommy. I'll have to ask Fifi to help me with using the round needles, if that is what they are called, since some of the women said they are hard to use. Worse case, I can watch a video on the Internet. You can learn almost everything that way."

I wish I could learn how to do fool-proof spells. "You are right."

"I realize it's still summer, but winter will be here before we know it, and I want my son to be warm."

Winter. Ugh. I shivered at that thought. Sure, it was Florida, but sometimes the cold wind would whip off the ocean like a stone skipping across the pond and chill me to the bone. "Tell me again who is in your group."

"There were five of us the first time I went. One or two were new to me. I did get the name of one woman. It was Genevieve Dubois."

I smiled. "Ooh. I like her name. Is she French, too?"

"I don't know. She doesn't have an accent. She seems sweet, though. I don't think she's ever knitted before either, because she's actually a worse knitter than me." Penny smiled.

Wait until I showed up. "Interesting. Where is she from?"

"I didn't ask," Penny said.

Really? Why not? Penny was not shy. Oh, well, to each her own, I guess. I had no such qualms asking fairly personal questions. "While I don't want to look like a fool and show everyone that I don't have a clue how to knit, I might have to put my pride aside and join you all. I love meeting new people and trying to figure them out."

She chuckled. "You just like to psychoanalyze them."

"There's nothing's wrong with that." I might have majored in math, but I also find people intriguing and complicated. And sometimes not what they appear to be.

After Penny finished telling me who else was in her knitting circle, we talked about how it was going between her and her beau, Hunter Ashwell.

She sighed. "I'm in love."

"Oh, Penny, I am so happy for you. I hope Hunter feels the same way." I bet her new makeup and enticing new scent were due to Hunter.

"He hasn't said. I believe it's because he thinks his ability to shift into a wolf will eventually turn me off, but that's not going to happen. Besides, it's not as if I haven't seen him in both his animal and human form before, and I'm totally fine with it."

"Be honest. We were both a bit freaked out the first time we saw men shift."

"True, but I've had time to get used to it. Maybe when Tommy gets a bit older, we'll tell him, and then Hunter will feel comfortable enough to tell me how he feels."

"That makes sense, but you should talk to him," I said. "Most men aren't good at reading people. Tell him that you accept him for what, or rather, who he is. It's not like he had a choice whether to be a werewolf."

She huffed out a laugh. "I know, but I'm not in a hurry. However, you're not one to talk. It's not like you've told Jaxson exactly how you feel."

"He knows I love him, though I haven't said those three

little words to him yet. When we took that three-day vacation to the Florida Keys, I think I made it clear that I loved being with him. Actions always speak louder than words, right? At least, that is what both my mother and her mother used to say." In my heart, I kind of knew that wasn't totally true.

"Has he hinted at marriage?"

For some unknown reason, chills raced up my arms just as my pink pendant heated up. I stilled. Was my grandmother trying to tell me to go for it, or was she remembering how we used to talk for hours about my dreams? "Not yet, but I'm not in a rush."

"You're twenty-seven. Times a ticking."

I laughed. "You sound like my mother. And besides, you're no youngster." She was almost thirty-four.

Penny grinned. "It's not like I need any more kids. Tommy is enough to handle."

Her eight-year-old was rambunctious for sure. Since we were discussing love lives, we went on to talk about how well the new candy store owner, Courtney Higgins, and her time-traveling new boyfriend, Dominic Geno, were getting along.

"Her store is doing well too," Penny said. "I think having the kids out for the summer is really helping her sales. Every time I walk by, there are people at the soda counter too."

Her shop had every kind of candy imaginable. My mother said there was candy from when she was young. "When the tourists come in the winter, she'll do even better."

"I'm sure, and it doesn't hurt that Courtney is pretty, bubbly, and a good businesswoman. With Dominic by her side, she can't go wrong," Penny said.

"You are so right."

We finished off our wine, chatting about everything

under the sun, including my lack of clients. I guess since Jaxson and I weren't trained in the traditional sense to be private investigators, we couldn't complain that we didn't have people waiting in line for our services. Most of the time we ended up helping the sheriff with one of his cases, especially if magic was involved. Thank goodness, we'd come into a large sum of money a few cases back, or we would have had to return to our old jobs.

She yawned and then stood. "This has been so much fun, but I've gotta go. Mom is babysitting Tommy, and I have the early shift tomorrow."

"I can still remember those days when I had to drag myself out of bed at six in the morning to serve breakfast at the restaurant." I hugged Penny goodbye and walked her to the door. "Later."

"We must do this again soon."

"Totally."

As soon as she left, a sense of malaise washed over me. I never realized how much I loved being around people. Now that we had no cases to work on, I was kind of lost. Yes, I had Jaxson, but he had a life, too.

Iggy crawled over to the door and looked up at me. "Do I have to wear that sweater thing?"

"I thought you loved it."

"It's pink."

Poor Iggy. "And half green. I really appreciate you telling Penny you liked it, though, but what's wrong with pink? You're pink."

"Oh, how the irony escapes you."

I cracked up. Iggy always could make me smile.

Chapter Two

I'D MANAGED TO roll out of bed the next morning at the early hour of nine thirty. Don't judge. I am a night owl. After washing up and blindly grabbing a top and a pair of pants, I was finally ready to greet the day. Yes, I had on a random pair of pink jeans, but in deference to my cousin, Rihanna, I put on my one black shirt—her favorite color. I shivered at how much I'd changed in this last year.

As I was heading to the kitchen to grab a much-needed cup of coffee, someone knocked on my apartment door, and my fogged brain failed to register that someone would actually need me this early in the day. Hopefully, it was someone knocking at my aunt's door across the hallway.

Another knock sounded. Guess not. It wouldn't be Jaxson, since he would have texted first.

"Coming," I called with a rather dry mouth. I pulled open the door to find none other than Steve Rocker. "Sheriff. This is a surprise."

Steve was a tall, rather handsome man in his mid-thirties. He'd served in the military, and maybe because he wasn't home as often as his wife had wanted, she'd divorced him—or so he'd claimed. A bit adrift, he came to Witch's Cove to find work here since his grandmother was the receptionist at the sheriff's department—and still was. There had been a recent opening, because the former administration had either been sent to jail or was dead—long story—and Steve applied for the job. Needless to say, he was hired.

"Glinda."

He didn't look particularly distraught, as he usually did when someone died, so I figured that meant all of our residents were still alive. Something must have happened, though, or he wouldn't be here. That meant he might need me and Jaxson to help him with a case. Dare I hope it involved magic?

"What can I do for you?"

"May I come in?"

I was a space cadet this morning. "Of course." I stepped to the side and motioned him in.

"Thanks." He eased down onto the worn, flowered sofa while I took the chair across from him. I would have offered to make him a cup of coffee—in part because I really needed one—but he always turned down my offers of a drink.

"What's going on?" I asked.

"I just came from the church."

It really was none of my business when or where he worshipped, though I suspected he'd gone there for another reason. "On a weekday?"

He lifted his hand. "There was a robbery there last night."

A robbery? That might be a first for the church. "What was stolen?"

In the past, the only crimes I even remembered being committed were by kids knocking over a few of the smaller grave stones in late October. That or they'd defaced a statue or two in the courtyard, but none of the crimes had ever needed my witchy expertise.

"The gargoyle on top of the church is missing."

"Oh, no. The last time that occurred was maybe fifteen years ago."

His brows rose. "Ben Miller never mentioned it had happened before."

"That's probably because he wasn't the reverend then."

"No, I suppose not. Did they find out who stole the gargoyle back then?"

I was surprised he hadn't put two and two together since he'd worked with Hugo, Andorra's gargoyle familiar. "I need to tell you a story."

He looked at his phone. "Will this take long?"

"Really? Okay, maybe it will, but it might solve your case."

Steve pocketed his phone. "Then I'm listening."

"Remember I told you that when a witch turns twelve, it is a rite of passage to go into the Hendrian Forest and say a spell in the hopes of being a host for a familiar?"

He looked over at Iggy. "Yes, it's how you got your pink iguana."

"Yes, and it's how Andorra got Hugo." I waited for him to put the pieces together.

His eyes lit up, and his brows lifted. "Hugo was the missing gargoyle from the church fifteen years ago?"

"Yes." I can't believe someone hadn't told him Hugo's history.

"Do you think that since Hugo became Andorra's gargoyle familiar that some kid went into the forest and did a similar spell yesterday? Instead of getting whatever it was he or she wished for, they ended up with the missing gargoyle?"

"It's possible. I'd ask Hugo if he knows anything about that statue, but, well, you know, he is in his stone state at the moment."

"Yes, and I also remember that Hugo only turns human-like when his host is in danger. Maybe we should threaten Andorra so we can ask him," he said.

"Possibly, but no telling what Hugo would do to you." Steve had seen Hugo in action and understood just how powerful he was.

"Hugo knows me. I doubt he'd harm an officer of the law."

I smiled. "True. In the same vein, he'd know you were kidding if you pretended to harm Andorra. When I get to work, I'll see if Jaxson wants to come with me to investigate this *theft*."

A hint of a smile appeared. "Don't you mean this potential *run away*?"

"I do, but do you think the reverend would ever believe that the gargoyles on his church can up and fly away?"

"That would be a no. He's convinced it's the act by some kids."

"I don't know Reverend Miller all that well, but I suspect he's not a fan of the occult. To be clear, you are asking Jaxson and me to look into this event since magic might be involved, right?" Not that the sheriff thought that when he came over.

"I didn't realize magic was involved—or rather might be involved—but I must have known on some level, because I instinctively sought you out." Steve smiled. "I'm glad I don't have to beg."

I laughed. "Never."

This should be fun.

As soon as Steve left, I gathered Iggy and headed over to our office. We had a case! Most likely, we wouldn't be compensated for our time since the sheriff kind of passed it off to us, but I think it would be exciting to solve this one, especially if that stolen gargoyle really turned out to be someone's familiar.

"Are we going to talk to Hugo?" Iggy asked. "I bet he knows about the missing gargoyle. He told me he spent years on top of that church."

"I realize that, but his church sitting was a long time ago. Besides, if you recall, your friend is a piece of stone at the moment. He's not human anymore, so I don't believe we can communicate with him. When I say *we*, I mean you and Andorra." Not that Hugo ever was really human since to be human, one needed to eat and sleep. Hugo did neither.

Iggy poked his head out of my bag. "I bet I can convince him to change."

I know that Iggy and Hugo had a special bond, but Andorra, Hugo's host, said that Hugo won't transform without cause. I didn't want to remind Iggy that he'd tried once before and failed. "We'll see."

When we entered the office, both Rihanna and Jaxson were there. I had to say, my boyfriend was looking good, though he would still be handsome if he'd just come in from digging clams all day and had sand and sweat covering his arms and face. His dark hair was carelessly finger combed back like he'd been battling a strong wind, and his distressed jeans with the few holes in them only added to his casual appeal. But I most appreciated his tight dark green t-shirt. He'd been hitting the gym a lot lately, and it showed.

Rihanna was sitting on the sofa reading, while Jaxson was at the computer doing his thing, whatever that happened to be at the moment. As far as I knew, we didn't have a new case.

"Whatcha all doing?" I asked as I placed my purse next to Rihanna.

Iggy crawled out of my bag and nudged Rihanna to get her attention. "We have a case," he announced.

Jaxson spun around. "We have a case?"

"Not a paying one." I told both of them about Steve's visit this morning and how the gargoyle on top of the church was missing.

"How?" Rihanna asked. "I've never tried to lift Hugo, but I'm betting a piece of stone his size would weigh a lot."

"I thought the same thing, but according to Steve, the reverend thinks it was kids."

"I'm with Rihanna," Jaxson said. "Stone is heavy. Carrying something down from the rooftop would require some significant muscle."

"Muscles like you have." I winked.

"All the more reason to doubt kids could have pulled off this prank."

"I agree, which makes me think it wasn't a prank." I told them my familiar theory, reminding them about how Hugo came into existence.

"That sounds more plausible. Want to head on over to the church and check it out? It would be helpful to know it wasn't a theft."

"I thought you'd never ask. Iggy or Rihanna, do you want to come?"

"Yes," they said in unison. I wasn't surprised that Iggy wanted to join us, but I figured Rihanna would have other things to do. Since she'd recently graduated from high school, she'd been spending her days either taking photos—her future career—or hanging out with her boyfriend.

"I thought you would be with Gavin," I said.

"He's visiting colleges, trying to decide between the University of South Florida and the University of Florida."

"Good choices. How long will he be gone?"

"Gavin and his mom will return tomorrow night."

"Nice. Ready to go?" I hadn't eaten breakfast or had my cup of coffee, but this was more important than my needs.

Since the church was about a mile away, we piled into my car and drove there. Given the hour, and the fact it was off season, the road was practically empty. When we arrived, I parked, got out, and looked up. Sure enough, the gargoyle on the right spire was missing.

"Is that empty space where Hugo used to live?" Iggy asked as I gathered him up and put him in my purse.

"No. He was the one on the left. At least, I think he was on the left. I can't remember when, but the church eventually replaced him. We'll have to ask Andorra to be sure."

Since it was a weekday morning, no one was around. We entered the empty church, and the smell of freshly polished wood pews filled the air. Religious statues might have lined the walls, but because there were no stain glass windows, I never warmed up to the place. My Aunt Fern, however, loved to come here. She said it gave her time to reflect. That probably meant she was there to talk to her husband, Harold, who'd passed away a few years back.

"The reverend is probably in his office in back," Jaxson said.

"How do you know where his office is?"

"It's just a guess, pink lady."

I didn't have a better suggestion, so we walked past the altar to the door on the far left hand side. Sure enough, we found Ben Miller hunched over his desk, squinting at some kind of ledger. He reminded me of Friar Tuck from those old Robin Hood movies—short, round, and with a bit of gray fringe above his ears.

He jerked when he saw us and planted a hand on his chest. "I didn't expect to see anyone today." He blew out a breath and smiled. "How can I help you?"

"We'd like to try to help you." I told him who we were, since I doubted he remembered everyone in town. I then explained about the sheriff's visit this morning.

"That's nice of you to want to help, but what can you do that he can't?"

I didn't feel comfortable telling him about talking familiars and how one of the gargoyles who'd resided on the church's roof for years was sort of human. "We're good at asking questions. People often don't want to say anything to the law."

"I see."

"Steve said you thought it was kids?"

"Yes. There are these four boys, troublemakers for sure, that have been coming in early for Sunday service and then lingering outside long after everyone else has left."

That didn't sound evil to me. Perhaps they were troubled youths looking for answers. I had taught school for a year, and I couldn't remember any kids who hung around the church. Sad, really.

"Maybe they find solace being in this sacred space." Yes, I know I sounded like my parents' daughter but being raised by a funeral home director had consequences.

"I doubt it."

"Did you give their names to the sheriff?" I asked.

"Yes, and he said he'd question them."

Kids would never confess unless Steve saw fit to threaten them with jail time. Even then, that tactic didn't always work.

"Do you think we can get access to the roof?" Jaxson asked.

"Sure, but why?" Reverend Miller asked.

"To see whether all or only part of the gargoyle is missing."

"Okay, but I wonder why the sheriff didn't ask to go up?" Ben Miller asked.

Good question. Thankfully, no one answered. The reverend pushed back his chair and motioned we follow him. At the end of the hall was a door that he yanked open. "Just go up the stairs. It will lead to the roof."

"Is this door always unlocked?" I asked.

"Don't see a need to lock it."

Why not? He was already suspicious of these boys. They could have snuck into the rectory, climbed the stairs, and reached the roof without Ben Miller noticing. The real question, though, was how could they have gotten down again carrying a heavy, awkward statue without anyone seeing them?

My devious mind pretended someone called the reverend away from his desk, but the only entrance to the church seemed to be at the front. If that was the case, there was no way they could have left unnoticed.

I followed Jaxson and Rihanna up the stairs that creaked and cracked with each step. I hoped none of them were rotten. It would be quite a long way down if the steps gave way.

From the smelly mold lining the stairwell walls and the occasional cobweb, it didn't look as if anyone had been up here in a long time. One of the four boys surely would have rubbed against the walls at some point, either coming or going, and I didn't see any smears from where a shoulder might have brushed up against it.

I coughed from the spores entering my lungs and then closed my purse to keep them from attacking Iggy. Thankfully, we reached the top quickly. As soon as I was outside, I sucked in a deep, cleansing breath of warm, sticky air. The tar paper covering the roof looked in need of repair—and a good cleaning—but the view of the ocean from up here was quite breathtaking.

Rihanna stopped, probably to admire the view. "I wish I had my camera with me."

"That would have been nice." She also could have snapped some photos of the crime scene, though Jaxson's cell took high quality photos.

We all walked over to where the gargoyle had been, and Jaxson ran his hand over the smooth surface.

"That is interesting," he announced.

"What is?"

Chapter Three

I LOOKED OVER at the space where the gargoyle had been sitting, but I didn't see anything odd about the area, other than the fact that the gargoyle was no longer there, and some seagulls or pigeons had been busy. "What do you think happened?" I asked.

"Unless the statue wasn't attached to the ledge, there should be some bolts lying around, or at the very least, cement dust, indicating someone had used a drill to remove them.

"They didn't break him off with a sledge hammer or anything," I said. "The surface is smooth."

Jaxson went over the other statue. "Lookie here, guys. This one is attached with metal bolts. I don't imagine the two gargoyles would be mounted differently."

Iggy poked his head out of my purse. "We really need Hugo on the case."

"I agree. We need to ask him how he got loose. The problem is that Hugo is in no shape—pun intended—to answer us."

"Aren't you funny. Can we visit him?" Iggy asked, sounding excited.

They were buddies, and I know how upset he'd been when Hugo transformed back into his statue form.

"We can ask Andorra, but I believe she told us that he's never appeared when spoken to. I'm sorry." It hurt me every time Iggy asked to visit his friend.

Iggy looked around. "This place is disgusting."

I wasn't sure what he was referring to. "Why is that? The view from up here is amazing. Do you want to see?"

"No. I'm not stepping foot on all of that bird poop."

I laughed. Just then two seagulls squawked and flew overhead.

"Duck!" Iggy yelled as he buried himself in my purse.

I'm never seen Iggy afraid of anything. "It's just a bird. You'd think you'd never seen one before."

He peeked his head out. "Are they gone?"

"More or less."

"They are nasty creatures."

"They're just seagulls—albeit noisy ones. They can't help where they go. You do realize they can sense if you don't like them. I've heard their aim is quite excellent."

He looked up at me. "You're making that up."

I swallowed a laugh. "Am I?"

"You'll pay for this," Iggy said as he went back to hiding.

I didn't have time to help Iggy get over his dislike for seagulls, because Jaxson returned after doing a perimeter search.

"I don't see another way down. It would be suicide to carry the statue down a ladder that was leaning against the wall. Do we know when the statue went missing?"

"No, but we can ask the reverend when he noticed it was gone."

"Assuming there were thieves, they would have had better

luck taking it in the middle of the night."

"That makes sense. The church is on the main thoroughfare. Normally, during the day, people are either driving or walking by and would see someone carrying a large statue, but this time of year? I'm not so sure. Let's hope the church has security cameras," I said.

"Doubtful, but we should ask."

"I think we should confer with Andorra," Rihanna said. "Considering how long it's been since Hugo became her familiar, he might have told her about his method of descent."

I tapped on my purse to get Iggy's attention. He poked his head out. "Are they gone?"

"Yes. Did Hugo ever tell you he could fly?"

"You mean like a seagull?"

I guess they hadn't discussed it. "Maybe not quite like a bird, but how else could he get down from atop the church?"

"He teleported."

"I forgot that he had that talent. I need to brush up on gargoyle-shapeshifting abilities, I guess."

Jaxson snapped a few photos with his phone, though there really wasn't much to see. "Let's head back down."

We asked the reverend when he first noticed the gargoyle was missing, but he said it had been a parishioner who had called him this morning to report it.

"When you came in yesterday, did you look up?" I wanted to know if the statue could have been gone for more than a day.

"No. I was too focused on getting my keys out to open the front door."

"When was the last time you saw both statues?"

The reverend dragged his fingers down both sides of his mouth. "I couldn't say."

"That's okay."

"Are there any security cameras near the church," Jaxson asked.

"Of course not. This is a place of worship. People deserve their privacy."

They also deserved to be kept safe. It would have been nice to have evidence of Hugo's twin being visible one second and then gone the next though. I would have to ask Gertrude if she'd heard of any new familiars in town.

We thanked the reverend and then told him we were stumped about the missing gargoyle, but that we weren't giving up. Next stop had to be the Hex and Bones Apothecary. If Andorra wasn't working today, I imagined we could find her with Drake.

With the car air conditioner once more cranked up to high, we drove back to town where I parked in front of the office. The short walk across the street and down a few stores had me sweating again. Why again did I love Florida in the summer? The humidity frizzed my hair and made my clothes sticky. Answer? I didn't much, but Iggy loved this time of year.

The inside of the occult store, however, was deliciously cool and smelled slightly of lavender and mint, scents that were both soothing and refreshing. Andorra was with a customer, so I walked over to Hugo. I lifted Iggy out of my purse and set him next to his friend. Since no one was around, I figured his presence wouldn't bother anyone. Besides, only a witch could hear Iggy's chatter. "Do your magic, little one."

He spun around and craned his neck. "I might be little, but I'm mighty."

I laughed. "Yes, you are."

As if Hugo were some dog, I petted his stone head. "I hope you and Iggy can figure something out."

I didn't have high hopes that Iggy could miraculously convince Hugo to reappear as a human and do a tell-all, but I could still wish it. Andorra's customer left, and Rihanna and Jaxson went over to her.

If I thought the ancient tomes of magical knowledge would have any information about gargoyle familiars, I would be pouring over those books in a heartbeat.

After I tugged down my shirt that had creased up in back from the car ride, I went to speak with Andorra, too.

She looked up when I arrived. "Jaxson and Rihanna were telling me that there might be another gargoyle familiar around?"

I didn't like that she sounded so surprised. "If you were able to summon one, couldn't someone else be able to do it?"

Andorra stared at me. "I have no idea. I guess they could."

"I trust there is no way you can ask Hugo, right?"

"I can ask, but he won't answer."

That didn't sound hopeful. "No amount of pleading with him will get him to reappear in his human form?"

She tapped her fingertips lightly on her lips. "Not that I know of, but I can try again. I'll have to wait until after we close, though." She chuckled. "I don't need some customer telling the town that a crazy person is working at the Hex and Bones."

"I totally get it. I'll ask Gertrude if she had a vision of

some gray piece of stone soaring through the sky or if she's aware of another gargoyle in town."

Andorra nodded. "It would be kind of cool if Hugo and this other gargoyle could meet, and it might not be for the first time either."

"Right, especially if they were next to each other on the church ledge for so long. Did he ever mention if he could communicate with other stone statues?"

"No, but I never asked him either. Hugo isn't the type to volunteer information," Andorra said.

"Supposedly, any meeting would have to be held here since Hugo never leaves the store, right?"

"Oh, he can leave, but he has no need to. Think of him like your laptop. You can leave it unplugged for a while, but then the juice runs out and needs to be plugged in. Consider his magic to be like the necessary power. That's why Hugo stays here, but it's not like he couldn't leave. Remember, he lived on top of the church for years."

"I hadn't thought about that. Did he teleport—or whatever it's called—from the top of the church to standing in front of you?"

"I was twelve. All I remember is that I happened to look up at the church and saw the statue missing. The next thing I knew, this twelve-year old boy is in front of me. I'm not sure I put the pieces together right away."

"I wouldn't have either," I said.

"Do you think Hugo used all of his reserve energy to get down off the church?" Rihanna asked.

Andorra looked over in his direction. "Can you believe I never asked?"

I might not have asked Iggy everything about his transformation from an ordinary iguana into a special one either. I placed a hand on her arm. "Let us know if Hugo spills the beans about his former church mate, if that is the right word."

"Will do."

After retrieving Iggy, we left. "I'd like to stop off at the sheriff's office," Jaxson said. "I imagine Steve will want to know if we learned anything about the so-called theft."

"Which we didn't."

"No, but I'll tell him what we suspect. And you? What are you planning next?" he asked.

"Like I mentioned to Andorra, I want to see if Gertrude can provide any insight." I looked down at Iggy, who was slumped in my purse. Poor baby. I really think he believed he could bring Hugo out of his cemented state. Hopefully, seeing Gertrude again would perk him up.

Jaxson turned to Rihanna. "And you?"

She shrugged. "I'm always up for seeing Gertrude."

"Then I'll catch you ladies, and gentleman, back at the office." Jaxson winked. Heart flutter time.

"Do you think Gertrude will know anything?" Rihanna asked as we crossed the street.

"I wouldn't ever count her out. If she has no idea about the missing gargoyle, I'd like to pick her brain about familiars in general."

"Not that I have time for one, but does a witch have to be twelve to get a familiar? I mean, could I try for one at my age—again, not that I want one."

"That's an excellent question. Neither my mom nor Aunt Fern have one. Andorra does, but why not Elizabeth or their grandmother?"

"And why not Gertrude?" Rihanna asked.

Iggy stuck his head out of my purse. "Why not me? I'm a warlock, kind of. Can I get a familiar?"

"You sort of have one in Aimee." That was a stretch, I know.

"She's a girlfriend, not a familiar."

I didn't want to get into that conversation. "We're here, so shh."

"You're no fun," Iggy said.

To my delight, Gertrude was available to see us. When we walked into her office, she must have just finished a séance because the sulfur smell of extinguished candles lingered in the air. The drapes were drawn to help make seeing any ghost that appeared easier, but that made the room dark and rather somber. If it hadn't been for the lit desk lamp, it would be hard to see in there.

Gertrude looked up and smiled, but despite the cheer, she looked tired.

"Welcome, ladies. Please excuse the séance table taking up lots of my office space."

"No problem."

"Did you bring your cute pink friend?" she asked.

Most likely she already knew the answer. Gertrude could sense these things. Iggy poked his head out of my purse. "Hi, Gertrude. I'm here."

"Iggy, my boy, come over here and visit an old lady." I lifted him out of my bag and handed him to her. She placed him on her lap. With all the folds in her skirt, he was nearly swallowed up in the fabric, but he didn't complain. She looked up at us. "Have a seat on the settee. How can I help you today?" she asked.

I was a bit stunned that she hadn't read Rihanna's mind. "There might be a familiar on the loose."

"It's a gargoyle," Iggy piped up.

Gertrude stroked his back. "Is that so? Tell me about it. I hope Hugo didn't run away."

"No. He's still at the Hex and Bones." While I was sure Iggy would like to tell her everything about the missing gargoyle, he would take forever, so I had to intervene. "We believe the gargoyle on top of the church became someone's familiar."

"Oh, my. I hadn't heard."

Was she slipping? Or didn't she want to show her hand? "Do you know anything about gargoyle familiars? And have you met Hugo?"

"I have not met Andorra's familiar, but you've mentioned his capabilities." She sipped the tea that had been sitting in front of her on the table. "Yes, yes, that might be something."

I had no idea what she was talking about. "What might be something?"

"I had a vision last night. Because it's summer, I thought the lightning was merely indicating we were in for a big storm."

Rihanna smiled. "But it wasn't about weather was it?"

My cousin must have read her mind. "In light of what you told me, perhaps not."

"I don't understand," I said.

Iggy lifted his head. "Hugo can freeze things. Maybe Gertrude's vision is about a gargoyle that can create lightning."

I smiled at him. Iggy was adorable, but sometimes naïve. It then occurred to me that maybe Hugo had told him about other gargoyles, though in all honesty, how many could he have met? From what Andorra once told me Hugo only remembers being on the church in our town. "Did Hugo say anything to you?"

"Not much," Iggy said.

I turned my attention back to Gertrude. "Do we believe that the missing gargoyle turned into a familiar to stop from being stolen? Maybe. The lack of any physical evidence like cement dust and screws on the church's roof implies he teleported somewhere," I said.

I waited for Rihanna, Gertrude, or Iggy to chime in. I didn't want to be unwilling to look at all avenues. I once more faced my familiar. "When you were trying to get Hugo to talk at the store, was there any sign of life coming out of him?"

"I don't think so."

Gertrude lifted Iggy up. "Are you sure? While I don't have a lot of experience in that field, maybe you felt some heat or an energy coming from him."

"I wish. I tried. I really did."

Poor Iggy. "I'm sure you did." I looked up at Gertrude. "Where do we go from here? It's not like we can do a séance or a locator spell for a statue." I clicked my fingers. "Or could Hugo?"

"Did you forget Hugo isn't in his human form?" Rihanna asked.

"I know." I turned to Gertrude. "Is there a spell we can do to bring Hugo out of his stone form?"

She smiled. "Find the missing gargoyle and you might solve your problem."

If we found our missing gargoyle, we wouldn't need Hugo to transform to do the locator spell. Or was Gertrude talking in code again?

Chapter Four

THE MEETING WITH Gertrude had mostly been a bust, except that Iggy was in a better mood afterward. Gertrude always seemed to cheer him up.

After we left her office, I suggested we stop at the diner. "I'm starving. I didn't have breakfast since Steve came before I even had my coffee."

Rihanna sucked in a breath and then grinned. "Glinda Goodall without coffee in the morning? Watch out world."

"You're a real comedian. Let me call Jaxson and have him join us. I am curious if Steve told him anything." I texted instead of calling in case he was still at the sheriff's department. He immediately texted me back saying that he'd come right over.

We walked the short distance to the diner and slipped into a booth. The heavy scent of fried onion rings mixed with a hint of chocolate, most likely from the shake in the booth next to ours, made my stomach grumble. Yum. However, I would be good and actually order breakfast instead of the shake that I really wanted.

Dolly Andrews rushed over, no doubt having heard about the theft at the church. She'd want to know any details we'd found out. "Did you hear?" she said, slightly out of breath.

Dolly was actually a bit disheveled at the moment, which was rather unusual for the neat owner. Wisps of her dyed blonde hair were sticking out of her hairnet, and her apron was a bit askew.

"Hear what?" I didn't want to give anything away yet.

"Last night, Fifi's Yarn shop was broken into."

Every muscle froze. "Say what? Tell me what you know."

She motioned for Rihanna to scoot over in the booth. My cousin picked up Iggy and handed him to me.

"Can we go look?" Iggy asked. My familiar did love a crime scene.

"Shh." Dolly couldn't hear him, and I always felt a little odd talking to my iguana as if we were really having a conversation, which, of course, we were.

"This morning when Fifi opened up, her place was a total mess. Someone had taken pink yarn and tied it from one corner to another, crisscrossing the whole store."

I partially wanted to cheer, because someone else loved pink, but at the same time I was horrified at the vandalism. "Does Steve have any idea who is behind this?"

"Not yet. Well, he might know, but Pearl hasn't found out anything, and I'm getting antsy for details."

I wonder how Dolly had found out this much? It was not even noon, so I doubted Fifi would have come across the street to the diner and told Dolly about it. From the way Penny described her, I didn't see the yarn shop owner as being pals with the older owner, though I'm not sure why I thought that.

I blew out a breath. First, it was the church theft—if that is even the right word—and now a store had been broken into. Wow. "Was there any other damage? Not that having to clean up that mess isn't bad enough."

"Not that I heard about," she said. "But apparently, Fifi is raging mad."

"I can't blame her," Rihanna looked over at me. "Should we go over and see if we can help clean up? I bet she'd appreciate it."

I knew why she was suggesting it. "I think that is a very neighborly thing to do, assuming our sheriff's department will let us in. You know Steve and his yellow crime scene tape."

"True." Because Dolly had been so forthcoming, I had to tell her about the missing gargoyle. Steve had asked us to see what we could learn, and Pearl would find out that we were helping with the case. She in turn would eventually tell Dolly. Then my wonderful gossip source would be upset that we'd withheld information from her. "Did you hear about the missing gargoyle on top of the church?"

"No, I haven't. What is Witch's Cove coming to? There never used to be any crime here."

Then the crooked deputy was murdered, and the town went downhill from there.

Just then Jaxson rushed in. He spotted us, smiled a knowing grin, and slid in next to me. "What did I miss?"

I briefly explained about the yarn shop being broken into. Since Jaxson had just come from Steve's office, he might have some details about what happened. "Did our sheriff say anything about that?"

"Only what Dolly told you. The strange part is that the cameras show no one going into the store. And get this—the locks appeared to be untouched."

I didn't want to consider that this was a repeat of the thefts that occurred last year. Those warlocks had opened locked doors with their minds. It was powerful, scary stuff.

"Maybe someone snuck in during the day and hid," I suggested.

Jaxson shrugged. "It's possible, but the store isn't that big. Even if someone managed to stay out of sight, the vandal would have to get out again. Remember the case we had like that?"

"Of course. I was thinking the same thing, but I hope it's not related. Dealing with those warlocks was a nightmare." They could cloak themselves and hide in plain sight. I looked over at Dolly. "This may sound crazy, but is it remotely possible that Fifi did this herself?"

Dolly chuckled and then sobered. "Why would she partially destroy her own store?"

"As a publicity stunt?"

"I've never heard of anyone doing something like that, but if it had been me, I'd have hired someone to break in—and hired them to clean up."

"Me, too," I turned to Jaxson. "Did Steve say whether Fifi was aware that there were cameras in the front and back?"

"Steve said that the building owner told Fifi and Courtney about them. They had the option of removing them in case they didn't want to pay the monthly fee to have them up and running," Jaxson said. "Apparently, Fifi never discontinued the service."

"I should probably have some installed," Dolly said, "but I've never had any trouble with theft or vandalism."

I looked over at Jaxson. "We should consider it at some

point, too."

He nodded and then looked over at Dolly. "How about we order? I'm starving."

She grinned. "Of course. What can I get you?"

I went with some much-needed coffee and scrambled eggs, but at the last minute tossed in the English muffin. I did love my carbs. Rihanna had fruit, coffee, and a sweet roll, whereas Jaxson stuck to black coffee and two fried eggs, over easy. The man had discipline.

"Any other information on the familiar idea from Gertrude?" he asked once Dolly took off to place our order.

I had to think if we learned anything. "Not really, other than she had a vision about an approaching storm. I'm not sure what that was about."

Iggy crawled up my arm and onto the table. "I still think the lightning is about our gargoyle."

"How so?"

"I already told you, but I have no proof."

I'm glad he was learning that having proof was a good thing. "Tell Jaxson what you told me." I'd kind of forgotten his logic.

"I'm thinking this new gargoyle might be able to shoot lightning from its hands just like Hugo can do with ice."

"I like it, buddy," Jaxson said. "The sheriff never mentioned anything about scorch marks, though."

"I wasn't suggesting the gargoyle was the vandal. I was just saying that the gargoyle has many talents, that's all. Sheesh. Pay attention, people." Iggy opened his mouth and wagged his tongue.

I chuckled as Jaxson petted Iggy. "Good sleuthing, buddy," he said.

Iggy crawled up Jaxson's arm. Those two had become so close.

"What's next on the agenda?" Jaxson asked me.

I told him that Rihanna and I were going to see if we could help Fifi. "Did you see any yellow crime scene tape across the front of the store when you came over here?"

"I did not."

"Maybe Rihanna and I can check it out then."

"I want to come," Iggy said.

I didn't think that was a good idea. I looked up at Jaxson, hoping he'd understand that Iggy could be more of a hindrance than a help. Iggy's claws would get tangled in the yarn too easily.

"Buddy, I need you to help me at the office."

He eyed Jaxson. I swear Iggy was getting good at seeing through a lie. "What can I do?"

"I want to do some research on gargoyles, and I'd like your input. You're the only one, besides Andorra, who's ever communicated with one."

"Okay."

Jaxson was the best. "If the Internet doesn't prove useful, maybe Levy can help." Levy Poole and his coven were very powerful and knowledgeable. "He might know how a person was able to get in and out of the yarn shop without notice."

The food arrived, and I couldn't wait to dive in. Without me remembering to ask, Dolly had added a small plate of lettuce for Iggy.

Jaxson sipped on his coffee. "I think asking for Levy's help is a great idea. How about giving him a call? I'm sure Iggy would like to go back and visit."

"Yes!"

I loved it. Problem solved. As much as I wanted to eat, I explained that I needed to step outside to contact Levy. "Too many ears are in here."

Jaxson smiled. "I agree. Good luck."

Once outside, I called Levy. I explained about the missing statue and then reminded him about Hugo and how he came from that same church. "I figure if Andorra did a spell to get Hugo, maybe someone ended up with the other statue."

"That's highly interesting. I can look into it. Anything else?"

"Because I'd like to give a hand to the owner of the yarn shop whose place was vandalized, do you think Jaxson could do a little research at your library? Iggy will help."

"Absolutely. I'm sure I can scrounge up a few people to do a bit of investigating. Gargoyle research will be a first for us."

"We've seen Andorra's familiar in action a few times. He is impressive." I explained that he was now in his statue form.

"I'm excited to check it out. I'll head on over now. Have Jaxson knock on the side door, and I'll open up."

"Thank you. I hope to repay you someday," I said.

"Nonsense. You bring us the best requests."

I chuckled. "I'm glad to be of service." Once we disconnected, I hurried back inside. My food was calling to me.

"What did he say?" Jaxson asked.

"He was very excited to help." I looked down at Iggy. "And he was particularly happy to see you again."

"Yippee."

"But I forgot to ask him about how someone could get into and out of the store without being seen. Maybe you could ask him. If Hugo wasn't in his stone form, I'd suspect him."

Most likely Levy would suggest it was a warlock with that particular skill.

"Hugo wouldn't do anything bad," Iggy said.

"I figured as much. Can you ask Levy about it though?"

"Maybe."

That was good enough. I looked across the street and had a brilliant idea. "What do you think about taking Andorra with you to the library? She's been dying to see the inside of the coven's vault room, and I promised her she could go. Only the last time, Levy didn't ask us to come over there."

"That's brilliant," Rihanna said. "She probably knows more about the abilities of gargoyles than anyone."

I agreed. "Precisely."

"I'll call her," Jaxson said.

That worked for me. I continued to eat while Jaxson spoke with Andorra. From the length of the conversation, our friend didn't need much convincing. "She's good with it?"

"Totally."

"Now that you've finished, head on out. It's my treat," I said.

He grinned, leaned over, and brushed a kiss on my cheek. "See you back at the office. Have fun untying yarn."

"Funny."

Once he left with Iggy, Rihanna and I finished our meals. Because the diner was filling up, I didn't want to linger. That would cost Dolly money. After I paid, we headed out, but not before I checked every booth. It was a habit I had yet to break.

I recognized most of the people, but it wasn't like the yarn destroyer would be here—or would they? While I wanted to stop and chat with a few of the patrons, we had work to do.

"You haven't met Ms. LaRue, have you?" Rihanna asked.

"No, but Penny has. According to her, Fifi is an angry woman and does not have the best social skills. And that's a direct quote." Or as close to it as I could remember.

My cousin scrunched up her nose. "That doesn't sound like someone who would want to open a yarn shop. I pictured someone who loved to sit and knit all day."

"Me, too. Like Pearl."

My cousin grinned. "Absolutely. Let's hope this Fifi woman isn't a witch who can block her thoughts, or we will have done a lot of work for free." She held up a hand. "I take that back. She seems like she's in need of help, and I want to be there for her. She is a member of our community now."

"True." I sucked in a breath. "I don't know why it never occurred to me to think she could be a witch." Not that she would tell us, even if I asked. I remember when I'd first met Courtney, the owner of the candy store. I didn't learn about her abilities for a while.

"It's possible that Fifi used magic to mess up her own store. A quick hand swipe and voilà! The place is a total mess."

"Let's hope not." I tugged on the front door of Fifi's Yarn shop, only to find it locked, so I pressed my face to the window. Wow. The devastation was extensive. It looked like a kid had fun stringing the pink yarn everywhere. Nothing was knocked over, nor were any shelves trashed. It was just a mass of yarn. The woman inside, who I assumed was Fifi, was frantically cutting away the pieces. She looked to be at her wits end, and my sympathy swelled. I knocked.

She stopped, looked up, and shook her head to indicate she was closed.

I inhaled. This might be more difficult than I'd anticipated.

Chapter Five

"WHAT DO YOU want to do?" Rihanna asked. "She doesn't seem to want us here."

"I disagree. She doesn't want to deal with a customer. We aren't here to buy yarn supplies. We're here to help." I pressed my face against the window again and tried to smile.

I must have drawn her curiosity, or perhaps it was her sympathy, because she finally opened up. The woman was stunning, but her pursed lips weren't all that attractive right now, not that I blamed her for being in a foul mood.

"I'm sorry, but someone broke into my store. I'm not ready to open." Fifi lifted her chin.

"I know. My cousin and I are here to help you clean up."

She stilled. It was as if she wasn't sure she'd heard us right. "That's not necessary."

I looked behind her. "Looks like you could use a hand. No strings attached, I promise. I'm not looking for any free yarn."

Her eyes watered. "Oh, okay. Thank you, *cheri*. Come in."

As soon as we stepped in, she relocked the door. I doubted whoever did this would return during the day, but I almost didn't blame her for being cautious. Of course, she could just want some peace from prying eyes.

The interior still had that fresh paint smell, and the colors surrounded me felt like I'd walked into a rainbow. I wanted to toss a bunch of skeins of yarn on the ground and fall asleep on them.

"I can't believe someone would do this. You've been here less than a month. Someone from your past has to have done this. The residents of Witch's Cove don't do this kind of thing."

Fifi lifted her chin. "Apparently, they do."

When I finally took my eyes off of the mess, I studied her. Fifi had dark brown hair pulled up into a French Twist, a hairstyle I thought had gone out of fashion years ago. I suppose if she believed most of her clients would be older, then it just might work. Her black silk pants were elegant, as was her cream colored blouse. Personally, I thought she looked like she was about to go out to a fancy dinner party rather than be at work, but maybe that's the way the French did things.

I probably should take a page out of her book and dress a bit more professional. After all, I ran a company, albeit one that didn't often charge for our services.

"You have no idea who would do this?"

"Laura Singletary."

I figured she'd say no, but instead she tossed out a name. That worked. I've never heard of this person, and I knew most of the people in town. "Who is she, and why would she want to do this?"

Fifi rolled her eyes. "It's so stupid really. Laura had the nerve to come to my first knitting club get together. I swear she was here to spy on me." Fifi waved a dismissive hand. "She's a short, bitter woman with wild red hair. I didn't like her at all."

So what? Red hair is a crime now? And what did her stature have to do with anything? Fifi might not be short, but her attitude was rather condescending, though who was I to say Fifi wasn't right? I'd have to ask Penny if she remembered this woman.

"Why would Laura want to spy on a newcomer?" Rihanna asked.

"*Ooh la la*. Because that woman has an imagination like no other. Her boyfriend lives down the street from me, and he volunteered to help me with one of the leaky pipes at my house. That is all. Next thing I know, she is coming to my knitting circle. Trust me. The woman doesn't know a skein from an old sock."

I was no expert either, but this didn't sound like someone who would be able to break into a store unnoticed. "Did she ask if you were seeing this boyfriend?"

"*Mais oui*, but I told her that Jeffrey was not my type. Just between you and me, his facial hair is quite scraggly. *Terrible*." The last word was said with a French accent, or at least that was what it sounded like to my untrained ears.

This motive seemed rather bogus. "Besides this jealous woman, anyone else?" Penny had told me that Fifi was divorced, but I couldn't see a man doing this. "Could someone else in your knitting circle not have liked the way you criticized one of their stitches? I know I am reaching, but I really am trying to help."

She stopped snipping the yarn. "Who are you again?"

I don't blame her for asking. A normal person wouldn't have been such a snoop. Besides, we never told her our names. "I'm Glinda Goodall, and this is my cousin Rihanna Samuels. My aunt owns the Tiki Hut Grill on the other side of the street. I grew up in Witch's Cove, and this type of behavior is totally unacceptable."

"Oh. I see. I am sorry. I have been quite stressed since opening my shop. I don't normally attack nice people."

"I totally get it," I said. "Rihanna and I came to help you clean up. That's all. I didn't mean to be so nosy." I wanted to touch my nose to see if it really had grown longer since I'd just lied. Big time.

"Thank you. I'll get you two some scissors. The yarn is a total loss."

Fifi LaRue went into the back and returned with them. As much as I wanted to look around for clues, neither of us moved. I also couldn't wait to hear Rihanna's take on her.

We spent close to an hour cutting and unknotting the yarn from around every artifact in the place. I couldn't imagine how long it took to do this prank—assuming magic wasn't used. And thinking of pranks, this was something a senior class in high school would do—or rather what my senior class would have done.

"How did this person get in, if you don't mind me asking?"

Fifi waved the scissors. "I don't know. The sheriff said he was going to look at the video feed. All I know is that when I came in this morning, my key slipped in easily. I have no I idea if I would even know if someone had picked the lock or not."

That sounded so much like the case with the warlock robbers. Was magic once more the cause? I was starting to get a bad taste in my mouth about warlocks. "They didn't leave a note?"

Her eyes widened. "What would it say? I hate you? Leave town?"

Ouch. That was harsh. "I don't know."

Rihanna stopped cutting. "Was someone planning to blackmail you? This act could have been a precursor to show you they were serious—that they had power."

Her jaw lowered, and I swear her face paled. "Power? No. And I don't have any secrets, so no one would or could blackmail me."

Everyone had secrets, which was why I didn't believe her. I could only hope that Fifi wasn't a witch who could block her thoughts. "Good to know. Did you loan your key to someone by any chance?"

"No. Never. The only one who has a copy is the owner, Mr. Richards."

I'd have to have a talk with Heath. Maybe something needed to be fixed in the store, and he gave the key to a workman.

As much as I wanted to ask about the ex-husband, I had already overstepped my bounds. I picked up the rest of the yarn ends from off of the floor, and when I looked around to see what else needed to be done, the store had been transformed.

Fifi set down her scissors and exhaled, looking like this terrible event was past her. "Thank you for your help. I'm not sure I could have finished without you both. It's all been so much."

I thought that was a tad dramatic, but I suppose if someone had done this to our office, I'd feel the same way. I really didn't think we'd been there very long. "We didn't do much."

"You did. Really. I want to thank you in some way. I should ask if either of you knit?"

"No, but maybe I'll give it a try some time," I said. "These yarns are so beautiful. While it is hot right now, it can get quite chilly in the winter."

"I know. I lived in the Panhandle for years. It was like having a real winter, except that it didn't snow—at least not often."

I was glad to see Fifi had a sense of humor. "Who knows? Maybe I'll see you on Sunday for the knitting circle."

She smiled for the first time today, showing that Fifi LaRue was a very pretty woman. "Thank you, again. Having the support means everything. The first skein and a set of needles are free for you both."

"Thank you." I honestly hadn't expected any compensation. It wasn't why I volunteered.

After that warm response, I almost wanted to hug her. Or did the French kiss on the cheek instead? Since I didn't know, I smiled and motioned to Rihanna that we needed to leave. I didn't need to say anything since my cousin was probably being bombarded with my thoughts.

We left, and I kept quiet until we were safely across the street. I stopped, needing to figure out our next move. "Wow. That was an experience."

"I could unravel every ball of yarn before I could untangle her mind."

I didn't like hearing that. "Do you think she's a witch?" The only person I'd heard of who could block Rihanna at will was Gertrude.

"I don't know. Sometimes it happens when the person is highly anxious."

"I vote for that option. Having her be a witch might complicate things somehow. Let's hope that Levy has given Jaxson and Andorra a few hints about the gargoyle at least. I need some good news."

"We could sure use some," she said.

"I'll text Jaxson and see where he is. If he's still with Levy, do you want to get an iced tea at the tea shop?"

She grinned. "That's the best suggestion you've had all day."

I laughed and then texted Jaxson. My phone rang a few seconds later. "Hi."

"Andorra and I just got back from Levy's. We're at the Hex and Bones. How was your clean up?"

"Interesting. We can meet you at the store, or would you care to join us at the tea shop?"

"I could use something to drink, but I'll be coming alone."

I couldn't tell what was going on. "What about Iggy?"

"Our little detective is convinced that he can draw Hugo out of his shell. I say we give him an hour and then pick him up."

I loved it. "Perfect. See you at Maude's."

I would have waited for him to cross the street, except that Jaxson had his car and would have to park in front of the office first.

When Rihanna and I entered the tea shop, the scent of the cinnamon scones on top of a layer of rose tea had my stomach grumbling. Cutting yarn had been hard work.

We grabbed a table, and I was curious to see if Maude would have some inside scoop on the pink yarn caper. She spotted us, smiled, and held up a finger, indicating she'd be right over to help us.

By the time she was finished with her customer, Jaxson had come in. "How did it go with Levy?" I asked.

"It was very interesting. His library is something else. I must have sneezed ten times, though. I don't think many of those books had been dusted in years."

I laughed. "You are right, but those dusty books are invaluable. Did the coven members find any information on gargoyle familiars?"

"Yes and no."

Maude breezed up to the table. "I am sorry to keep you waiting. What can I get you?"

We told her what we wanted. I thought she'd leave, but she just stood there. Hopefully, that meant she had information for us about the yarn incident at Fifi's shop. I thought it best to toss the ball in her court. "Did you hear about the mess at the yarn shop?"

"Yes. It's such an awful shame. Who would do this?"

From the twinkle in her eye, I had the sense she had some suspects. "I don't know. Rihanna and I just came from helping Fifi clean up, but she was at a loss as to who might have vandalized her place."

Maude pulled out the fourth chair and sat down. "I heard Samuel Dickens was quite upset that he didn't get to rent the space. Maybe he did this."

"Isn't he the vice-president of the bank?" Jaxson asked.

"Yes, he is. He doesn't like to publicize it, but his wife is slowing down. She has a lot of aches and pains and wants to quit working at the bank. She thought opening her own yarn shop would help keep her mind off of her condition."

My heart sank. "I am sorry she's not doing well." I didn't know what else to say.

"Me, too. Apparently, Heath Richards banks with him, and because of that, Mr. Dickens thought that Heath would lease the place to him. Only Sam forgot to sign some papers or something, so when Fifi came to town and paid six months' rent in advance, Heath took it."

Wow. That was really convoluted. "You're saying you think that portly Mr. Dickens, who looks like he is suffering from gout, broke into the yarn shop and strung pink yarn from top to bottom?"

"I didn't mean he'd personally do it, but he really wanted this for his wife."

"I get it," I said. "Let's hope something comes to light soon."

Maude dipped her chin, probably trying to look stern. "You let me know if you learn anything."

"I'm sure Pearl will find out what's going on before I do. Rihanna and I just went over to help her clean up."

"Pearl doesn't know much other than the fact that Steve thinks it's kids."

That might have been what he told Pearl. "It looked like a high school prank for sure."

High schoolers, however, might not have the sophistication or ability to get in and out of the store without being seen on camera. Hmm. I had to believe a witch or warlock was involved in some way. But for what purpose? I doubted this stunt would be enough to get Fifi to close up shop after only being open less than a month, especially if she'd paid six months in advance.

Why did the plot always thicken just when I thought I was getting a handle on things? One of these days, we'd get an easy case.

Chapter Six

Once Maude seemed satisfied that neither Rihanna, Jaxson, nor I knew much about the vandalism, she left to make our order. It was disappointing she couldn't add much. Though knowing that people were clamoring to rent the yarn shop was good for Heath Richards. I would be curious to know how Fifi had the money to buy all of the yarn supplies from the former owner and pay six months' rent. Was it possible she received the money in her divorce settlement, or was she a rich woman in her own right?

Right now, I was more interested in learning about gargoyles. "Tell me about what Levy's coven found out."

"There is nothing specifically known about gargoyles, but there are several speculative pieces. Unfortunately, they seemed to contradict one another."

"How so?" Rihanna asked.

"Some books claimed that certain species of gargoyles possessed their own internal power. That means they are free to roam at will. They don't need some occult store to give them their strength."

"Like Hugo does," I said.

"Yes. Similar to humans that have good people and bad people, gargoyles can be good or bad. The good ones are protectors," he said. "I'm thinking Hugo would fit into that category."

"For sure. Did any one of these books indicate when or how a gargoyle decides when he or she should shift into their human form?" I asked. "Is it only when danger is present?"

"That was unclear. None of the coven members found any spells to draw gargoyles like Hugo out of their stone form. It's apparently up to him whether he changes or not."

I sank back into my seat. "Don't tell Iggy that. He'll think Hugo doesn't like him."

One of the servers delivered our food. The cinnamon scone I'd ordered teased my senses and made my mouth water. "Thank you."

I dove into my dessert. It wasn't that I was disappointed in what Levy's group discovered—or hadn't discovered—but it would have made things easier if I could have learned more about how gargoyles came into being and how they transformed. These beings fascinated me.

"Was there any mention as to why a gargoyle would be a person's familiar verses a cat or an iguana?" Rihanna asked. "Andorra never asked for one."

"No. I was surprised how little was known about familiars in general. Since many witches, and I'm guessing warlocks, can have them, there should be more information about them. Only there wasn't."

Suddenly my scone didn't taste as good. "What I'm hearing is that we have no clue what happened to the gargoyle on top of the church, and we have no idea who vandalized Fifi's shop."

"That about sums it up. Did Fifi tell you anything else? I

had the sense that you were hiding something from Maude," he said.

I stilled. "You are almost turning into a mind reader like Rihanna."

She laughed. "In his dreams."

"Let's just say Glinda has tells," Jaxson said. "When she touches her necklace, it means she is hiding something,"

"What are you talking about? I touch it when something reminds me of my grandmother." As soon as I said that, I wasn't sure if that was true or not.

"See?" Jaxson nodded to my hand.

I lowered it. "I didn't even know I was doing it." He smiled, and I had to chuckle. "Fine." I told him who Fifi suspected.

"She thinks her neighbor's girlfriend is jealous? Why not just confront Fifi and tell her to back off? Are women really that passive aggressive?" he asked.

I had to think about that. "Some women aren't good at confrontation. I think we need to focus on who could have gotten into and out of the store without notice."

Rihanna sipped her tea. "That's the same question we asked about the gargoyle. How could the thieves have reached the rooftop and then gone down again without anyone seeing them?"

Okay, that was deep. "Are you saying there is a connection? That some cloaking warlock is doing this—and by this, I mean stealing a statue and messing with Fifi's store?"

Rihanna looked over at Jaxson, though it wasn't like he'd know.

"Anything's possible," Jaxson said. "Since we have to

return to the Hex and Bones to pick up Iggy, I say we ask Andorra if she has any ideas. The yarn shop break-in and the theft do have some similarities."

"Sounds good, but I'd like to sit for a few minutes and enjoy my snack. Sometimes, not having to figure out a puzzle helps my mind refresh."

For the rest of our tea time, we talked about how Rihanna's photography was coming along. She was working on creating a strong portfolio before she started college in the fall, which wasn't far off.

"I'm happy with my photos, but at some point, I might have to leave our small town for a change of scenery," she said.

My fingers almost crushed the paper cup. "For how long?"

She grinned. "For the day. Don't worry; I've come to love Witch's Cove. I'm not moving."

"Good." Thankfully, she was going to a junior college close by.

Once we finished and paid, we crossed the street and headed to the Hex and Bones. "How about we stop in Broomsticks and Gumdrops first to see how Courtney and Dominic are doing?" The candy store was next to the Hex and Bones shop. It was possible my need to stall was due to the fact that I wasn't ready to see Iggy sad because Hugo wouldn't change for him.

That aside, the candy store was special to us. In order to change what happened years ago in the store, Jaxson and I had somehow been transported back in time. That, however, was only after Dominic arrived in Witch's Cove from 1973. Very strange and complicated stuff. Dom was staying with Jaxson at the moment until he got on his feet. Thank goodness he was rather adept at computer programming, even if it was at a rudimentary level, because that helped him learn technology faster. Fifty years was a lot of time to catch up on.

"I'm game," Rihanna said.

"Me, too," Jaxson chimed in.

Inside, Courtney was with a customer at the cash register, but I didn't see Dominic. While she was finishing up, I checked out her offerings. I was a sucker for anything new. A minute later, Courtney came over.

"Hi, you guys. I haven't seen you in a while."

We'd stopped in for a soda about three days ago. "We're working a case."

"Fifi's yarn issue?"

"Yes. Have you heard anything?"

She shrugged. "I heard that her ex-husband came sniffing around."

Fifi hadn't mentioned him. Why would he come around unless he hoped to get back together? "I take it the divorce was amicable then?"

"I kind of doubt it. I heard that Fifi doesn't want anything to do with him."

"Interesting. Maybe he cheated, which was something she could never forgive." Or he was providing her with so much alimony that she couldn't afford to take him back? And if they got back together, she might have to return to north Florida and give up her store that she seemed to love.

"Sounds reasonable," Courtney said.

Dominic emerged from the back. "There you are!" I said.

From the slight dirt on his face, coupled with his untucked shirt, he'd been doing some heavy lifting in back. "I thought I heard you guys out here. How's it going?"

"Good. We caught a case." Or two.

"That's great news. Jaxson's been a little testy of late. He doesn't do well when he has nothing to work on." He grinned.

"I have not been testy," Jaxson shot back.

Dominic laughed. "If you need any surveillance done, I'm your man, assuming I can borrow a camera."

Rihanna nodded. "I have an older one you can use."

"Really? That would be great."

"At the moment, no surveillance is needed, but we will keep you in mind for when we do."

"I'd appreciate it," Dominic said.

Jaxson placed his hand on my back. "We promised Iggy we wouldn't leave him at the Hex and Bones for too long."

"Right."

"No problem," Dom said. "I have to get back to work anyway. I'm unpacking and cataloguing all of our inventory, and I can't take too long of a break. I have a tyrant for a boss."

Courtney looked up at him with moon eyes. "You are so silly."

"You two are adorable." I turned back to Courtney. "If you hear any good gossip, send it our way."

She hugged me. "You bet."

We left and went next door to the Hex and Bones. When I walked in, I abruptly stopped. "Uh-oh."

Jaxson stepped in front of me. "Let me find out what is happening."

"Iggy is with Hugo, so he'll protect him. The petite woman they are with looks like she couldn't harm a fly." The fact Hugo was in his human form meant danger was nearby, though.

The door behind us opened, and Drake rushed in. "Where is she?"

I turned around. "Who?"

"Andi. She called me. She is worried something bad might happen."

My mind had to unscramble all of this input. "Because Hugo changed form?"

"Yes."

I looked around. "Ask Bertha. Andorra is probably in the back."

"Good thinking." Drake took off.

I turned back to Jaxson and Rihanna. "Maybe Iggy was able to draw him out." Though why he would be successful this go around, I don't know.

"Let's go ask," he said. "It's a bit suspicious if we just stand in the entrance."

All I wanted was to make sure that Iggy was safe. As soon as I approached, Iggy spun around.

"Hugo is back!"

"I can see that. What's going on?" I didn't want to come right out and ask who the woman was, but hopefully, she could tell us how and why Hugo had transformed—assuming she knew.

The mystery woman was in her late twenties, early thirties with absolutely perfect skin. It was as if sun had never touched her face. She'd pulled back her long, dark wavy hair into a ponytail, showing off her perfect bone structure that looked as if someone had sculpted her.

Wait a minute. An idea formed, albeit a crazy one. I stuck out my hand. "Hi, I'm Glinda Goodall, and this pink honey is Iggy."

"Oh, we met. Iggy and I have been chatting up a storm."

If that was true, it meant she was a witch. Or was she more than that? I turned to my familiar. "Can you tell us what happened?"

"Sure. I thought you'd never ask."

Wasn't he sassy? "Tell me."

"I'd spent about a half an hour trying to convince old Hugo here to come out and play." Iggy looked up at him, waited a few seconds, and then nodded. He turned back to us. "Hugo said it wasn't his fault that he had to remain a statue. He said that he hadn't been able to shift back until after Genevieve showed up."

Genevieve? That name sounded familiar. "My good friend Penny mentioned you, unless there are two Genevieve's in town. Were you at Fifi's knitting circle recently?"

As if a bank of storm clouds had arrived, her face darkened. "I was."

Her reaction was rather telling. While I wanted to get into that tangled web, I needed to understand her relationship to Hugo first. I had a suspicion I knew what it was.

"Do you want to go someplace more private?" she asked.

You had to be kidding me. She could read minds? It was hard enough living with Rihanna, though my cousin was very good at not invading my thoughts unless it was necessary.

"That would be good." I picked up Iggy. "Hugo, will you join us?"

He nodded. Several people had come into the store and were looking at us for some reason. My voice must have risen. Whoops. Jaxson led us into the back room. I gave Bertha a small smile, and she seemed to understand what was going on.

As soon as we stepped into the back, Drake straightened.

"It's cool, Drake," Jaxson said. "Just a slight misunderstanding."

"We thought it would be better to talk in here," I said.

As if someone had just inflated her lungs, Andorra pulled back her shoulders. "Great. Let me set up some chairs."

Drake and Jaxson helped her. When they were placed in a circle, we sat down. Before Andorra took her seat, she closed the door. That was smart since I had the feeling that whatever Genevieve was about to tell us shouldn't get out in public.

"Thank you for welcoming me," Genevieve said.

I wasn't sure we had, but maybe she expected us to be hostile. "How about telling us about how you are able to communicate with Hugo?"

She smiled. "I've been waiting to tell my tale for many, many years."

This was going to be so exciting. "Please do."

Genevieve chuckled. "I'm not sure where to begin."

"Tell us how you met Hugo," I suggested.

"That's easy. We were both gargoyles on top of the church." She lifted her chin as if to challenge us to say we didn't believe her. The thing was, I did.

Hugo placed a hand on her arm, implying he was telling her something. "Oh, yes. Hugo reminded me that I should mention that I was the first gargoyle on the church. There was another one there before Hugo, but that was just a cement statue, carved by some artist."

I was a bit speechless. "And you weren't?"

Genevieve planted a hand on her chest. "No! Hugo and I were formed from magic, just like your Iggy was."

Formed by magic, huh. I bet I'd hear him repeat that only a few thousand times. "Okay, so when did Hugo arrive—if that is the right word?"

"A few years after I'd already been summoned to be a familiar."

"You're a familiar?" Iggy asked. "Like me?"

"Yes, but I'm hardly like you. You have a host who loves you. Mine rejected me."

Jaxson clasped my hand. He understood how much that would upset me. "Why? You're…perfect," I said.

She laughed. "Far from it. The girl who said the spell from the Hendrian Forest wanted a black cat. Instead, she got me."

I could relate, but the moment I saw Iggy, I fell in love with him. "Did she say she wanted to return you for a better one or something?"

"Not right away. I wasn't in my human form at first. Since it's kind of hard to pretend to be a familiar when I look like I'm made from cement, I turned human and have mostly remained that way. Barbara's friends thought I was just some visitor without any power. I never wanted to show them that I was different, which I think upset Barbara a lot."

"Then what happened?" Rihanna asked. She was leaning forward on the edge of her seat.

"Barbara put up with me for a while, but it became more and more clear that she didn't want me. She was twelve, and because she was young, she'd whine all the time because I wasn't a cat."

"Why do witches always want cats?" Drake asked.

"I'll tell you later," I said. "Though I'm thrilled I have Iggy."

My familiar looked over at me but didn't say anything snarky for a change. "Then what?" I asked.

"Then one day, Barbara told me I had to leave."

I sucked in a breath. "Did you look like a twelve-year old girl?"

"Yes. When I realized I wouldn't be given a second chance, I returned to the church tower. Either they hadn't noticed I was missing, or they just hadn't gotten around to replacing me, because I returned to my spot and transformed. I stayed that way until a few days ago."

A few days ago? Clearly no one had noticed until today.

"How tragic. Where is Barbara now? Do you know?"

"You bet I do."

Chapter Seven

"BARBARA AND HER family remained in Witch's Cove until after she left for college at Florida State."

"That's a college in the Panhandle area." I only mentioned it in case someone like Iggy didn't know.

"Yes. It was there that she met a man, got married, and then divorced him about six years later."

My spidey senses were going crazy. I didn't dare ask how Genevieve knew all of this. Had she teleported around Florida and kept an eye on her host—a host that had rejected her? If so, she must have done it at night when no one would have noticed her gargoyle statue was missing from atop the church. Just as I was about to ask her where Barbara was now, Jaxson asked a question.

"You mentioned that Barbara is from Witch's Cove. What is her last name?"

"Lipton or rather Lipton Simons after she married."

"I knew a Barbara Lipton in high school," Jaxson said. "In fact, she tutored me in…French."

"I knew it," I blurted. "She changed her name to Fifi LaRue, didn't she?"

Genevieve's eyes widened. "I have to say I am impressed, though Hugo did brag how smart you all are." She looked over at Iggy. "And your cute pink iguana is too."

The pieces were coming together. "Thank you. You were on top of the church before Hugo showed up, right?" She nodded. "Did he replace the old gargoyle?" I couldn't understand how this all worked.

"In a way. Do you remember the day you were born?" Genevieve looked around the room. Everyone shook their heads. "It's like that."

I was hoping they were different from regular humans but apparently not.

"Did you and Hugo become friends after he arrived?" Andorra asked.

Genevieve looked over at him. "Not at first. Hugo was too shy, but at night, I would transform into my then seventeen-year-old self and coax him out to play."

I was having a hard time with this. "You grow old like humans?" I don't know why I asked. Hugo had grown older.

"We can. I pretended to look like a teenage girl, hoping to attract his attention."

"Wow. Who named you? Andorra said that Hugo already knew his name."

I swear she blushed, though I knew that wasn't possible. Or was it? Genevieve seemed to be almost a different species of gargoyle, like Levy's coven had learned about. For starters, she could talk, and she seemed to be able to go wherever she wanted. She didn't need some occult store to provide her with energy.

"I named myself. My host gave me a name I didn't like, and once Barbara ditched me, I decided to pick a different one."

"I wish I'd have thought of renaming myself," Iggy said. "I would have picked something else."

I was a little hurt. "You don't like your name?"

He lifted his head. "It's unoriginal."

Now wasn't the time to hear his suggestions. "I don't really care for my name either, but you don't see me changing it."

Iggy glanced over at Hugo and then back at me. "Hugo says he'll call me Ford."

"Why Ford?"

Iggy tilted his head. "Duh. You know my hero is Harrison Ford. I often tell Hugo about his movies."

"I like it. It's nice to have such a wonderful friend." I still planned on calling him Iggy. I faced Genevieve, needing to get off that topic. "Since Barbara loved everything about France, I would have thought you'd want something different. Why pick Genevieve Dubois? It sounds very French."

She sighed. "It is. In the short time I was with Barbara, I fell in love with France, too."

"Did you name Hugo?" Andorra asked.

"I did."

"Why no last name?"

She shrugged. "Hugo fit. Who needs two names when there were only two of us on the roof?"

She had a point, except why did she give herself a last name? "Since you were at the knitting circle, I trust you can remain in your human form for as long as you want?"

Genevieve leaned over and stroked his arm in a loving manner. "Yes. We are slightly different species, but if Hugo is with me, he can draw his power from me. It's like I'm a solar panel, and he can recharge off of me."

"Can Hugo become human whenever he wants now?" Iggy asked with hope in his voice.

Our newcomer smiled. "You'll have to ask him, but I think the answer might be yes—as long as he lets me stay around."

All of this was mind boggling. "If it's not too personal, where do you live?"

She smiled. "Here and there. In that respect, I'm like Hugo. I don't have to eat or sleep, though I can if need be. In a social setting, I am often expected to take a drink, so I do. As far as where I'm planning to live, I'm hoping to visit Hugo often." She looked over at Andorra.

"Visit away."

"Thank you."

Wait a minute. If she'd only just come down from the church, how did she know about taking a drink during a social setting? Her timeline was way off, unless she was talking about her pre-teen years.

Come to think of it, how was she able to go to the knitting circle and have no one notice she wasn't on top of the church? In reality, most people walk by a tall building without looking up. It was also possible that she created a fake image in her place. But if she could do that, why not put one up there permanently? Ugh. I wasn't grasping this stuff at all.

Jaxson placed a hand on my bouncing leg, and I stopped moving. "Genevieve, why appear now?" Jaxson asked. "Why did you wait so long, especially if you knew that Hugo—someone you care about—has been here for years?"

That was an excellent question.

"It's simple. Barbara, or rather Fifi—which is a ridiculous name for a grown woman—moved back to town. I thought it was time to confront her."

I clamped a hand over my mouth. "It was you, wasn't it?"

She giggled. "Whatever are you talking about?"

"You vandalized the yarn shop to get back at Fifi for dumping you. I bet you can cloak yourself like Hugo can, can't you?"

She patted her face in a dramatic fashion pretending to be embarrassed. "Why yes, I did. As for cloaking myself, I can. No harm, no foul though, right?"

Except that Rihanna and I spent time cleaning up, but I wouldn't be surprised if Genevieve knew that. "If the sheriff finds out, what are you going to do?"

One second she was seated in the chair and the next she was nowhere to be seen. Genevieve was like Hugo. He must have not liked the loss, because, he too, disappeared. I glanced over at Iggy. Probably to show solidarity, he cloaked himself.

"Come on, guys, it's not funny," I said.

Iggy reappeared, but he was in the same place as before while Genevieve and Hugo were in the corner. Clearly, if she were ever put in jail, she could get out.

"Tada!" she said. "From what Hugo has told me, he is very talented. While I can't encase hands in magical ice, I have my own abilities."

"Can you create lightning?" Iggy asked.

If the color could have drained out of her cheeks, it would have. "Not exactly, but close. How did you know?"

I didn't want Iggy to make up something. "Our psychic, Gertrude Poole, had a vision of lightning. Iggy figured that it might have something to do with you."

"Oh." The two gargoyle-humans returned to their seat. "I might have to meet this amazing woman."

"I'm sure she'd love to talk to you." And pick your brain.

There was so much more I wanted to know, but right now, I was trying to assimilate what Genevieve had already told me.

On the surface, she seemed sincere. I would most certainly ask Rihanna her impression, but I had the sense that gargoyle mind reading wasn't in Rihanna's wheelhouse.

Genevieve turned to us. "Should I turn myself in?" she asked.

It wouldn't do any good if Steve couldn't keep her locked up. "I suppose it would be nice to have the question of who vandalized the yarn shop off his books. While you're at it, you could tell Steve you're the missing gargoyle."

She laughed. "He'd believe me?"

"It would be easy to show him, right?"

"Sure. I could transform from human to statue and then back again."

"Why did you do it?" Drake asked. "Vandalize Barbara's store, that is."

Hadn't I just given a good explanation why? Drake must have wanted to hear it from her directly.

She dipped her chin. "I think it is obvious. Or was my action too passive aggressive?"

How did she learn that psychological concept? She didn't have much parental guidance, and she'd only been roaming around for a short period of time. "It might be best if you talked with Fifi or rather Barbara first and explain how her rejection made you feel. When we spoke, Fifi was pointing her finger at a lot of people, but not at you."

"That means she didn't recognize me when I was at the knitting circle." Genevieve lifted her chin in apparent victory.

"I guess not." I had to believe my sixth grade teachers would still recognize me. I didn't think I'd changed all that much between twelve and twenty-seven, but maybe I had.

Genevieve stood. "I've decided that I want this cleared up. I will turn myself in. When your sheriff realizes that he isn't able to restrain me, he'll give me a stern warning not to do that again, and I'll go free."

I thought she'd been willing to speak with Fifi first.

"How about Glinda and I tell Steve that we found the gargoyle, and that this said gargoyle wanted to play a prank on her former host?"

"Would you do that for me?"

"Steve will believe us more than you. He'll probably ask you to come in, however, but we'll say you'll return to your gargoyle state, so he need not bother."

She grinned. "I could go back to the church. I don't mind. I like it up there. I get to watch people, and the view is great."

"Hugo would miss you," Andorra said.

"I know."

I looked around the room to see if anyone else thought that running away might not be the best idea. "What if people see that the gargoyle is back? It might cause a lot of questions."

"Hmm. You have a point," she said. "Since I've just reconnected with Hugo, how about if I talk to Barbara to see if maybe she won't press charges?"

"Sounds good. I need to ask you something. If you've been a stone gargoyle for most of your life, how would you know about the law, or how to read, or buy clothes for that matter? Did you look at fashion magazines at some point?" She looked so put together.

She laughed. "Oh, my dear Glinda. It's the power of magic. We just know these things." She pressed a finger to her lips. "As far as my wardrobe, I watch all of the people who come to church, and I get my cues from them."

That made sense, but how did she pay for her clothes? She probably conjured them. While her explanation was hard to believe, I had no other idea. Magic it was.

"Will Hugo change back once you leave the store?" Iggy asked, sounding rather desperate.

She lifted him up and placed my familiar on her lap. "No. I've done a little spell to help with that. In fact, he could come with me to speak with Barbara—or rather Fifi—but I think she might not appreciate having to go through me to translate."

As if the matter was settled, Genevieve stood and handed Iggy to me. "It's now or never."

"Good luck," I said.

"Thank you." She leaned over and kissed Hugo on the cheek.

Okay, I hadn't expected that. What was in line with my expectations was that Hugo just sat there. I hoped that his reaction didn't disappoint Genevieve. It was as if he didn't care if they were together or not. Then again, he might have spoken with her telepathically.

As soon as she left, I really wanted to talk about what had just happened, but with Hugo in the room, it would be a bit awkward, so I painted on a smile. "I guess both cases are solved." I turned to Jaxson. "Once we hear back from Genevieve, we'll speak with Steve and let him know he can close both cases."

"Great," Jaxson said. "But I'm not so certain Barbara will be all that forgiving."

"It's not like she has much of a choice," I said. "Pressing charges won't do any good. Barbara should know that."

"Maybe, maybe not."

We all stood. Once Andorra assured us she'd call once Genevieve returned, the four of us headed out. Iggy had spent a fair amount of time with Hugo and Genevieve, and I was hoping he'd be able to add something to my understanding.

By the time we reached our office, I was rather drained. "I need a tea. Can I get anyone anything?"

"Got any flowers?" Iggy asked.

I smiled. "Did you work up an appetite communicating with Hugo?"

"You understand! Yes. It's hard work."

I chuckled. "Anyone else?"

"Tea for me," Rihanna said.

"Water is fine," Jaxson chimed in.

I went into our makeshift kitchen and fixed the drinks. Since the hibiscus plants were in full bloom this time of year, I actually had some stashed in the refrigerator. I fixed our drinks and carried them out.

I placed the drinks on the coffee table and handed Iggy his hibiscus flower. He grabbed it, and then lifted one corner closer to his eye. "What is that?"

"What is what?"

"This is seagull poop."

Really? I checked out the flower. "It came from our bush, but we do live on the Gulf, and seagulls are all over the place."

"I bet Tippy heard me complain about the mess he made on top of the church and is out to get me."

Good thing I hadn't been drinking my tea, or it might be dribbling down my chin. "Tippy? Wherever did you get that name? And please don't tell me this seagull talked to you."

"No. He's not special. I named him Tippy because he's all white but has black tipped wings."

"He or she sounds pretty."

"Maybe, but it doesn't matter."

My curiosity got the best of me. "How do you know Tippy was the one who messed up your hibiscus flower?"

Iggy turned his head so that his eyes weren't facing me. "I just know. He's the leader. He's always first in line when flying."

This whole conversation was ridiculous, but Iggy seemed upset, so I didn't want to brush him off. "Would you like me to wash it?"

"Then the flower will get soggy."

"Fine. Go outside and get a new one for yourself."

He lifted his chest. "Excellent idea. I'll make sure to watch for Tippy. Just so you know, I really wanted to call him the poop master 5000, but I figured you'd be upset."

Iggy had finally lost his mind, but he was funny. I hoped his agitated state was due to hunger. "I would have been. Now go and get a clean flower to munch on."

"Fine." Iggy waddled toward the door and disappeared through the cat door.

Alone at last. "Rihanna, could you get a read off our new mystery woman?"

"I wish. She's not human. I can't read Hugo's mind either."

That was a little disappointing. "Magic aside, what are your thoughts?"

"I liked her."

"Yeah, me, too," I said. "And that worries me. To basically cover a store in yarn isn't a sign of a mature person. Though in truth, Genevieve isn't like the rest of us. It's possible, she might not know that her behavior was inappropriate." I huffed out a breath in frustration. "Where do you think these gargoyles learn the difference between right and wrong? And please don't say they are born with that knowledge. I'm not sure I believe everything Genevieve said about it being pure magic."

I looked between them, but no one answered.

"Is there anything else we need to do?" Jaxson asked. "So far, we know what happened to the missing gargoyle, and we know who teleported into the yarn shop and pulled a prank."

That might be true, but I was still feeling a bit unsettled. "All we can do now is wait for Andorra to call and let us know how the meeting went between Genevieve and Fifi. I'm going to agree with Jaxson. I don't anticipate it going well."

It was about an hour later when my phone rang. "I bet that is Andorra." When I looked at the caller ID, my stomach plummeted. "It's Steve." I answered. "Sheriff."

"Glinda, we have a problem."

And I could bet what it was. "Does it involve pink yarn and a missing gargoyle?"

"It does. Can you come over? I need a referee. Genevieve is out of control."

"Sure. We'll be right there."

Chapter Eight

I DISCONNECTED AND looked over at Jaxson.

"I take it Fifi wasn't too happy with her familiar's return?" he asked.

"I think not. I'm sure you heard that Steve wants us to talk with Genevieve, though I thought she was going to let us speak with Steve first."

"I don't think Genevieve always plans things out before she acts," Jaxson said.

I laughed. "You are right about that. She never had any parents to speak of nor was she given much guidance. I'm surprised she's done as well as she has."

Jaxson stood. "Let's see if we can salvage this situation."

"I want to go," Iggy said.

"Why?"

He looked around. "Genevieve likes me. If she does anything to make Hugo look bad, I'll tell her off."

I guess it wouldn't hurt. Steve couldn't hear him anyway. "Sure. Come along."

"I'll join you," Rihanna said.

"Great."

I didn't think Steve was expecting the four of us to descend on his office, but that's what happened. Genevieve stood the moment we entered.

"Hi, guys," she said.

"Genevieve." I would ask her what the problem seemed to be, but Steve would explain it better. First, though, I wanted to hear about her interaction with Fifi. "How did the meeting go between you and Barbara?"

"Terrible. She was mean. It was like I was twelve all over again—or rather she was twelve all over again. Time isn't really a big thing for me."

"I'm sorry. I was hoping you two could patch things up now that she is no longer a child."

Genevieve crossed her arms. "That might have happened if I hadn't wrecked her store. That was a dumb thing to do."

She was a bit harsh on herself. "You didn't wreck it. Once Rihanna and I helped, we were done in less than an hour. Mind you, the yarn was a total loss and had to be thrown out."

Steve cleared his throat. "Glinda, please sit down."

I might have gotten a little carried away. I was pleased he had enough chairs out this time, enabling the three of us to sit. Iggy thankfully decided to remain in my purse—for now.

"Genevieve here tells me she is the gargoyle that was on the church," Steve said. "Can you corroborate that?"

"I think I can, mostly because she has the same abilities, more or less, as Hugo. She didn't show you that she could shift?"

"No."

I looked over at her, and she shrugged. "It takes some energy to change, and I didn't think it was necessary."

That made sense. I turned back to Steve. "Did she tell you

about her history with Barbara Lipton Simons, aka Fifi LaRue?"

"She did. Genevieve confessed to the prank. I spoke with Fifi, or rather Barbara, but she wants restitution."

Genevieve shrugged. "Like I said, it didn't go well."

So she claimed. "In light of what you did, paying Barbara back is a reasonable solution. You ruined a lot of yarn, but I need to ask if you can pay her back?"

"With what?"

Surely, she knew what money was. "How about with dollars?"

She nodded, and instantly a wad of cash appeared in her palm. Genevieve held it out. "Is this enough?"

I was speechless. I had no idea if it was real or fake. Okay, it couldn't be real since she'd magically produced it, though it was possible she'd teleported into a bank vault, taken the money, and returned without us being aware of it.

"It is more than enough. Why don't you give it to Steve so he can count it for you?" And check the serial numbers to see if the money was counterfeit. If it was real, though, wouldn't that be worse?

"Okay." She handed it to him.

For someone who had acted with a great deal of sophistication before, she sure was being rather childlike.

"Where did you get the money, Genevieve?" Steve asked.

"From a bank. Isn't that what people do?"

From a bank. "Did you teleport inside the vault and take it?" I asked.

"Yes."

"That's not right, Genevieve." I tried not to be too harsh,

but she had stolen money.

"Why? It was there."

I looked up at Steve. He was the professional. Let him explain it to her.

"Genevieve, I have to give this money back. You need to earn the money."

She laughed. "Earn the money. How?"

"It's too bad we don't have factories in Witch's Cove, or you could work on an assembly line. You never have to sleep or eat. An employer would love to have you."

She grinned. "Maybe I can work at the Hex and Bones. All I really need is enough money to pay back Barbara. How long will that take?"

I liked her attitude. "I don't know. First, let's see if Bertha is hiring. Then we can see how long it will take you."

"Okay." And then she was gone.

I looked up at Steve. "Sorry, I didn't expect her to leave."

He waved a hand. "That's okay. It's better if she isn't here."

"You're probably right." I was aware she could cloak herself, which meant she could still be in the room, but I had the sense she had returned to the Hex and Bones.

Iggy poked his head out of my purse. "I want to go to the Hex and Bones to see Hugo. He needs to understand what is happening."

Rihanna pushed back her chair. "I'll take him."

Iggy lifted his chest. "I can go myself."

I feared someone might trample him. Not everyone looked where they were stepping. "You know you don't like it when a lot of people take your picture. You are kind of a celebrity."

"Fine."

Rihanna smiled and picked up Iggy. "Let's go chat with Hugo." She turned to us. "I'll warn Bertha and Andorra about Genevieve's request for a job, if she hasn't already hit them up for it."

"Thank you," Steve said.

Once my cousin and Iggy left, I leaned back in my chair. "Now what? Genevieve had no parents to guide her. I don't think she is a malicious person, but sometimes she does stuff that isn't smart."

"I can see that. I need to be able to tell the reverend something. Any suggestions?" His jaw tightened, implying he had a ton of other questions, but he wasn't certain he was ready to learn all of the answers.

"It would be great if Genevieve could create a lookalike statue, but I think that might prove more problematic." I wasn't sure she could, but I wouldn't know until I asked her. "Or just tell Reverend Miller that it's a cold case, and that you'll continue to work on it. I don't think the truth will help."

"Maybe not. I know I can't put Genevieve in jail—ever—but she needs to be held accountable. I'll talk to her and tell her that she is banned from visiting Fifi's Yarn shop. Ever."

"I think she'll be okay with that," I said.

"Did either Hugo or Genevieve ever mention that there were more gargoyles around here?" Steve asked.

"I hope there aren't. It might scare people. I've seen some of their capabilities, but I suspect they can do even more. Genevieve mentioned there were different gargoyle species, and that even within the same group, they have distinct talents. She wasn't any more specific than that."

"That makes them harder to deal with," Jaxson said.

"It does. Since there are werewolves roaming about town, and yet few know about them, we should ask Genevieve not to tell anyone that she and Hugo are gargoyles," I suggested.

"Good idea," Steve said. "Other than teleporting, mind reading, shapeshifting, and stealing money, what else can she do?"

I thought that was plenty. "I don't know. Genevieve seemed very open when she told us how she ended up on the church roof, but I believe she's holding a bit back. For now, I hope she helps Hugo enjoy life some more."

"By taking him for a walk?"

"I'm not sure what it all entails. I do know that she's had a crush on him for years, so I'm sure she'll take good care of him. Don't worry. I'll ask Andorra to keep an eye on Genevieve, but anyone who can teleport possesses a lot of power."

"That's what I'm afraid of."

"We just need to make sure she remains on our side."

"Let's hope," Steve said.

With that, we left, and headed back to the office. While Rihanna couldn't read Genevieve's mind, she was good at reading people in general, a trait she'd inherited from her FBI dad.

Once back in the office, I plopped down on the sofa. "It's going to take days to assimilate everything that Genevieve told us."

"You should give Levy a call," Jaxson said. "I bet his coven would appreciate a little tutorial on what Hugo and Genevieve are capable of."

"You're right. I can do that." I called Levy and told him what I could remember—which wasn't everything. Just then, Rihanna and Iggy returned, though I couldn't tell if he was happy or not. "I'm talking to Levy about what happened," I told both of them. "Anyone want to join in?"

Iggy perked up. "Me!"

I put the phone on speaker so that Rihanna and Iggy could fill in the pieces that I'd forgotten. "We're all here. Sorry."

"No problem. How did Genevieve act when you two went back to Hex and Bones?" Levy asked.

"She wasn't there, and Hugo was sad," Iggy said.

"Do you know where she went?" Goosebumps traveled up my arms. I didn't like that she hadn't returned to the store. After all, she said she planned to ask Bertha for a job. Did her word mean nothing?

"No," Rihanna said.

Jaxson held up a finger. "Hold on a sec, Levy." I looked up at him. "You want to add something?"

"While you're explaining things, I'm going to take a quick drive over to the church to see if Genevieve went back there. Not that I don't trust her, but she might be feeling a bit overwhelmed what with being rejected again by her host. Be back in a flash."

I nodded and then returned to my phone conversation. "Jaxson is headed to the church. He thinks Genevieve might decide to hole up on top of the church."

Levy chuckled. "I bet that will confuse your reverend if he

finds her there."

"I know, right?"

"Well, thanks for the update. Let me know if anything else happens. I might have to take the time to visit the store. I'd love to meet both of them."

"They are…interesting."

"I have to be there," Iggy said, sounding very important. "Only Andorra, Genevieve, and I can communicate with Hugo."

"I'll be sure to let you know if I visit, Iggy. Again, thanks."

I disconnected. "Phew. Is anyone else's mind blown?"

Rihanna held up her hand. "Me. At first glance, Genevieve seemed so put together. She's sweet, and she adores Hugo. While she claims she knows about the law, she isn't aware that taking other people's money from the bank is illegal."

"Do you think that Genevieve is playing us? Or isn't she aware what she's doing is wrong?" I asked.

My cousin shrugged. "I don't know."

We chatted about Hugo and Genevieve until Jaxson returned. I looked up and smiled. "Does the church have its statue back?"

"No, so I stopped back at the Hex and Bones, and they haven't seen her either."

I'm sure it was my imagination, but it seemed as if my necklace heated up for a moment. I looked down at the stone and caught the tail end of it glowing. "Nana?" I asked.

Not that I expected to see her ghost, but she seemed to be around when I really needed her. Unfortunately, she wasn't any longer.

I needed something to take my mind off this mess. "Who's up for an early dinner?"

"I am," Jaxson said, "but how about we take a little road trip to say Ocean View, instead of staying in town?"

"Too many prying eyes around here?" I asked.

"That's my take."

"I'm going to stay here," Iggy said.

When he turned his eyes away from me, I figured he was up to something. "No, you aren't. You're coming with us."

"Why? How would you like having to sit in a smelly purse for a few hours?"

"Smelly? If it stinks, it's because you've dragged dirt into it." I studied him. "Why do you want to stay here? If it's to see Hugo, forget it."

"Why?"

We'd been through this before. "It's too dangerous to cross the street."

"I know, which is why I'm going to see if Aimee will come with me. I'll ride on her back. I know that in order to be safe, I have to press the button to make the light change."

"I'll take him back," Rihanna said.

"You were just there."

Iggy lifted his chest. It was a defiant move. "I know, but Hugo wasn't being very chatty before. I think he just needed time to figure things out. I hope he knows more now."

I didn't like seeing Iggy disappointed if Hugo remained silent. "You're sure, Rihanna?"

"Yes," she said. "Besides, I want to give Gavin a call, and this will give me a chance. Even though he's coming home tomorrow, I miss him."

Aw, young love. "Okay, but you need to eat, too."

"Don't worry about me. I'll grab something at the Tiki Hut."

I wanted Iggy to be happy and turned to him. "I hope you find out something juicy for us."

He lifted his head. "Don't worry. I'm the great detective Iggy Goodall."

I had to swallow my laugh at that. "You are."

"I'll text you if Genevieve returns to the Hex and Bones," Rihanna said.

"That would be great." I wrapped an arm around Jaxson's waist. "Come on. Let's eat."

Chapter Nine

THE RESTAURANT THAT Jaxson took me to was on the Gulf of Mexico and had both an indoor and an outdoor seating area, just like the Tiki Hut Grill. Lights from the boats winked and skimmed across the surface like fairies, weaving and bobbing to the point where they mesmerized me. The air was delightfully warm and not nearly as muggy as it usually was during the summer months.

The best part about eating outside was the smell of salt mixed with a hint of seaweed. It reminded me of growing up when Dad used to own a small boat. On the weekends, we'd go fishing. I didn't catch much, but it was fun.

"Inside or out?" the waiter asked.

"Definitely out," Jaxson said. He understood how much I loved the mélange of ocean scents and the beating of the waves against the shore.

Once we were seated, I was finally able to relax. Even though we'd discussed the events of the day on the way over, my mind remained in turmoil, unable to think clearly.

"Why do you think Fifi, or rather Barbara, was so adamant about making sure that Genevieve paid for the yarn? I mean, it couldn't have cost all that much. Of all people, Barbara would know that Genevieve isn't a real human, and that she didn't receive the guidance growing up—thanks to her," I said. "I would think she'd be aware that Genevieve probably has never had a job and couldn't pay her back." I hated when I babbled, but, as I said, I had a lot on my mind, and I was still trying to sort through everything.

"Hard to say what the shop owner is thinking. After all these years, you'd think that the business woman would have gotten over the fact that she didn't get her cat familiar. If Barbara wanted one that badly, she could have gotten a rescue kitty."

I had to smile. "There is a difference. Can you imagine having Iggy if he couldn't talk or understand anything?"

"It definitely wouldn't be the same."

The waiter stopped by to give us our menus, and my mouth watered at the incredible array of seafood offerings. After scouring the menu, and changing my mind a dozen times, I finally decided on the shrimp Alfredo.

We ordered, and to my surprise, Jaxson added in a bottle of wine.

"Are we celebrating solving the case?" I asked.

"Can't I just enjoy a night out with my girl?"

"Absolutely." Jaxson Harrison was the sweetest man alive. I was feeling a bit unsettled, and his gesture calmed me. I had promised myself that I would try not to discuss the case for at least an hour, but I failed. "Did you ever look into Fifi LaRue?"

"I did, but I didn't get anywhere, which isn't a surprise since it's a fake name. Tomorrow, I'll do a bit more investigating into Barbara Lipton Simons, though if she's divorced, she might have dropped that last name. Why the interest? We know who vandalized her store."

I shrugged. "I don't know. I guess I want to know why I was getting a strange vibe from her."

Jaxson's brows rose. "Do you think that she saw the two of us together and worried you'd call her out for changing her name?"

"That sounds reasonable. I would be worried if I were her. I guess I should ask her why she chose to come back to Witch's Cove where she might be recognized? She probably hasn't changed all that much." Though Jaxson would know.

"I haven't seen her, so I couldn't tell you."

"She's elegant, pretty, and rather sophisticated."

He chuckled. "Then no. Barbara was none of those things in high school."

"Then I'm happy for her."

Our server returned with our bottle of wine. I always liked how the restaurant poured a bit of wine for Jaxson to taste. I guess that since his brother ran a wine shop, Jaxson had picked up a few tips about what was good and what wasn't. Me? If I liked the taste, I considered it good.

Once Jaxson gave the okay, the server poured our wine. "Your meal will be up shortly."

I smiled. "Thanks."

Jaxson held up his glass. "I don't know the exact date, but I think it's been about a year since we started our company. A lot has happened since then."

He was about ten weeks off with his date, but that was okay. I was thrilled that he remembered. "It has, hasn't it? Cheers."

We tapped our glasses and smiled. I then sipped the robust red wine, and the fruity flavor was a perfect complement to the salt air and warm Gulf breeze. Soft music was piped over a speaker—loud enough to be enjoyed, but muted enough to talk over.

In retrospect, I'd changed a lot over this last year and also had many new experiences. I fell in love, time traveled to the 1970s—twice—and solved numerous murders. Phew. Life had not been boring since Jaxson breezed back into Witch's Cove and into my life.

"Give me your take on our gargoyle situation," he said.

I lifted my glass to my lips to give myself time to think. "I'm worried."

His forehead creased. "Why? I know you trust Hugo."

"I do, but Genevieve seems a bit...unstable."

"I have to agree. Got any ideas what we can do to get her on the right path—assuming she is trainable?"

I had to think about that. "When I taught middle school, the kids who were the most troubled were often the ones who were seeking approval."

"Are you saying you think Genevieve trashed Barbara's store in order to get her attention?"

"Maybe. As they say, negative strokes are better than no strokes."

Jaxson whistled. "I hadn't thought of that. When Barbara didn't open her arms in welcome, that might have set Genevieve off. We should talk to Andorra tomorrow. Maybe she can shed some light on the situation."

"Let's hope. Of course, it might be a gargoyle thing. Hugo is a strange person, but I guess if I were mute and spent most of my time as a statue, I wouldn't have the best outlook or the best people skills."

"No, but do you think he'd ever pull a stunt like the one Genevieve did?" Jaxson asked.

"No, I don't. I wish I knew more about her. I'd love to pick Fifi's brain about what Genevieve was like when she was twelve, but I have the feeling our yarn shop owner won't be receptive to the idea of sharing. Her own actions wouldn't put her in a good light."

He smiled. "I think you are right."

"There has to be something we can do, though, to ensure that something like this doesn't happen again. If Genevieve did steal money from the bank, she has to learn that is unacceptable."

"Assuming she doesn't have her own safety deposit box with money that is legitimately hers, what do you propose?" he asked.

That was a hard one. "Maybe we can encourage Hugo to spend time with Genevieve in order to give her a bit of confidence. If she believes someone cares, she might think twice about doing something that is illegal, and we can suggest she pass things by Andorra first."

Jaxson dipped his chin, looking impressed. "I'm betting if you enlist Iggy's help, that might work better."

"That's a great idea."

Our meals arrived, and my stomach rejoiced. This was going to be a meal to remember.

THE POUNDING ON my apartment door the next morning

had me instantly alert. When I opened my eyes, Iggy was on my bed watching me.

"Who is it?" I was positive he knew. Iggy often would slip partway out of the cat door and check it out.

"The sheriff."

"Huh? What time is it?" I glanced at the clock. "Seven in the morning? Are you kidding me?"

I would have asked Iggy to tell the sheriff that I'd be right out, but they couldn't communicate. I pushed off the covers and slid my feet onto the floor. Since I didn't have time to dress, I tossed on my robe, and as I rushed out of the room, I cinched my sash tight. I then answered the door. "Sheriff," I announced as if it was an everyday occasion that he showed up at my door at the crack of dawn.

He strode in. *Come on in!*

"Where is Genevieve?" he demanded before looking around.

Did he think she'd be here? "How would I know? Try asking Barbara. She might have given her tirade yesterday some more thought and decided she wanted a familiar after all."

"Barbara is dead."

I had to grab onto the back of the chair to keep from dropping to the ground. His announcement took me totally by surprise. "Dead? How? When?"

"Some passerby spotted her in her store as they were getting their morning coffee. The medical examiner will be able to tell us when, but the knitting needle sticking out of her body implied that was the way she died."

I wanted to know the details, like where was this knitting

needle? That might give us a clue as to whether the person came from the front or from behind.

Thank goodness, Elissa was a fast worker. We might know the time of death by this afternoon. I walked around the chair and sat down. Iggy crawled over. He'd been asleep by the time Jaxson and I finished our romantic dinner, mostly because we took a late night stroll on the beach afterward.

"Did Genevieve say anything when you spoke with her last night?" I asked my familiar.

"She wasn't at the store when I showed up."

I told Steve what Iggy said. "You went over to the Hex and Bones last night, right?" I know Rihanna said she'd take him, but sometimes things go astray.

"Yes, but only Hugo was there." Iggy bobbed his head, probably to avoid me having to translate everything.

That must be true since Rihanna said she'd text me if Genevieve was there. So far, I hadn't received any message. "Did you ask Hugo where she might be?"

"Of course I did. He said he didn't know."

I looked up at Steve. "Hugo didn't know, but considering how those two seem connected, I'm not sure I believe him."

"How about you get dressed and we go over there?" Steve suggested, or rather, commanded.

"They don't open until nine, but I can call Andorra and ask her to meet us."

He nodded. "You do that. Please."

I called Andorra, and from the scratchy sound of her voice, I'd woken her up. "Sorry to get you out of bed, but we have a problem."

I explained what Steve had told me. "Do you know where

Genevieve is?"

"You think she did this? She's not a killer."

I figured she'd defend her, in part because Hugo was Andorra's familiar. "Steve thinks Genevieve might know something."

That was a little white lie, but in all honesty, that is what he might have been thinking.

"I have no idea where she is."

"Okay. Do you think you can meet me and Steve at the store in say twenty minutes?"

Andorra hesitated for a moment. "Sure. Elizabeth is out of town visiting family for a few days, and it's Memaw's day off. I need to get to work early anyway."

"Thank you. We'll see you there."

I disconnected. "She said she'd meet us there."

"I'll let you get dressed." He looked down at Iggy. "Meet me there, and be sure to take our interpreter with us."

I tossed him a brief smile. "Andorra can talk to Hugo, too."

"I know, but Iggy will make sure the conversation is accurately stated."

Wow. That implied he thought Andorra might lie. I wasn't awake enough to fight that battle. "Sure."

As soon as Steve left, I called Jaxson and told him what happened. "That's terrible. Do you want me to meet you at Hex and Bones?" he asked.

I always was more centered when he was there. "I'd like that. I just need to dress. I'm going to grab a to-go cup of coffee from downstairs. Want some?"

"I had some already."

We were so different. I liked the night, and Jaxson liked the early morning. "See you there then."

I didn't pay much attention to what I put on, except that I grabbed my pink sneakers at the last second. Once I gathered Iggy, I went downstairs for some coffee.

"Glinda! What are you doing up so early?" That surprised comment came from Aunt Fern who loved to be up bright and early.

Since she'd find out as soon as Pearl came into work that the owner of the yarn shop was dead, I needed to tell her. "Please keep this on the down low for a few hours, but Fifi LaRue is dead."

"What? Who killed her?"

Did my aunt seriously just ask me that question? "How would I know?"

"Well, I spotted Steve going up to your apartment. I thought maybe he was there to arrest you or else tell you who he suspected."

Me? Kill someone? I don't know what she'd been drinking, but I was not a violent person. "He asked for my help." I didn't need to mention that magic might be involved. It was kind of implied. "I'm meeting him over at the shop now, so can I get a cup of coffee to-go, as well as some lettuce for our little friend?"

She leaned over the counter. "Hi, Iggy."

He poked his head out of my bag. "Hey, Aunt Fern. I'll stop over later to give you the scoop. Glinda isn't telling you everything."

I so wanted to strangle him right now.

Chapter Ten

WITH MY HOT coffee in hand, and a few lettuce leaves for Iggy, I walked as fast as I could across the street to the Hex and Bones without spilling my drink. I know I let my aunt believe that I was going to the yarn shop, but Steve wouldn't allow anyone around a crime scene, which was why we were meeting down the street.

I hustled toward my destination. Since I didn't see Jaxson, Steve, or Andorra, I figured they might already be inside. I looked through the glass front door and spotted the group with Hugo, so I went in. I was thankful he hadn't retreated into his stone form. It was reasonable to think he might since he wouldn't have any reason to believe Andorra was in danger.

"Hey." I walked up to Jaxson.

Without prompting, Iggy crawled out of my purse and went over to Hugo. "Do you know where Genevieve is?" he asked.

Hadn't he already questioned Hugo?

Iggy turned around. "He hasn't seen her."

"When Andorra went missing, we did a locator spell, and Hugo, you were able to mentally communicate with her. Can you do the same with Genevieve? We think she might know who killed her host."

He shook his head, though I wasn't all together certain he was telling the truth. Even if Rihanna, my lie detector cousin, were here, she wouldn't be able to tell either.

I turned to Jaxson. "Maybe we should drive by the church again. She could be there."

"She wasn't yesterday, but I'm game to check it out again."

"Good."

"Glinda, who do you think is our best source for information for finding a runaway gargoyle?" Steve asked.

It was interesting that his grandmother wasn't his first choice. Most likely, he'd already called her, only to find out she didn't know. "Other than Andorra and Hugo, I'd say Penny. She was in the knitting circle, which started like two weeks ago. Genevieve was also one of those members."

"Where is Penny now?" he asked.

"At work. She gets off at three. Would you like us to come over when she finishes for the day?"

"That would be great."

"What about the ex-husband?" I asked.

"What about him?"

Weren't all ex-husband's suspects or was Steve still focused on finding Genevieve instead of the killer? "Courtney said he'd stopped by the yarn shop, but that Fifi wanted nothing to do with him. Maybe he harmed her." I wanted to give Steve a person other than Genevieve to focus on.

He pressed his lips together, clearly thinking about it. "It could be something, or it could be nothing. It's possible Barbara was afraid her ex would tell the world she wasn't French. If her store brand was built on that identity, she could lose some customers if people found out she was a fraud."

"I guess. I'll ask Penny to write down a list of names of those who were in the knitting group. Penny couldn't remember all of them when I asked her before, but maybe she's had time to think of who was there. I'm betting some of the women might be able to give you the rest of the missing names."

"That would be great. Thanks."

"Have you told Heath Richards yet about Barbara's death?" I asked. Heath owned the building. After his father passed away a few months back, he'd been given several strip malls. He'd already had to close down one because of his father's poor business decisions. Had it not been for a Witch's Cove fundraiser, these stores might have gone under.

"I haven't yet, but I will. There is only so much I can deal with at once. I don't think he is involved, but he will need to be told that he now has a vacancy to fill."

"I agree." It was a shame. Fifi's yarn shop was a great addition to the town. Maybe now Mr. Dickens will rent the place for his wife, so she'll have something to keep her busy.

I turned to Iggy. "Come on. We need to find Genevieve."

He looked back at Hugo. "Bye."

When Iggy lowered his head, my heart broke once more. "We can visit Hugo whenever you want. If Genevieve is correct, he can stay in his human form now." I didn't add that I believed he needed Genevieve to keep him that way.

I picked up Iggy, told Steve we'd be in touch, and then hugged Andorra goodbye. Without discussing the case, Jaxson, Iggy, and I crossed the street. I asked Jaxson to drive since my mind was going a million miles an hour. Could

Genevieve have killed Barbara? If she had, it wouldn't be with a knitting needle. Hugo had a lot of talent, and I suspected Genevieve might have possessed more than him. If that were the case, she'd have also used magic, not force.

The trip to the church didn't take long. As soon as I spotted the empty slot on top of the church where the gargoyle used to reside, I sagged against the seat. "She's not here."

Jaxson put the car in park. "Let's check the roof."

"Why?"

Iggy poked his head out of my purse. "Sometimes you just gotta trust the men."

His sincerity had me barking out a laugh when nothing else about the day had been funny. "Sure."

I didn't look forward to climbing those creaky steps or inhaling the toxic mold that lined the walls of the staircase, but in a desire to be thorough, I would do it.

"What are we going to tell the reverend about why we need to check the roof again?" I asked.

"We can say Rihanna left something up there."

I dipped my chin. "You want to lie to a preacher?"

"Do you have a better suggestion?" he asked.

"No, but I'd feel better saying we wanted to see the crime scene again. Maybe we missed something."

He nodded. "Let's do that."

Our luck, the reverend was nowhere to be found. I wasn't sure where he was, but I wasn't about to look for him. I was pleased he'd arrived early today and opened up. Most likely, he was praying in another part of the church.

The door that led up to the roof was unlocked. I still

thought he'd be smart to secure it.

The steps creaked even worse than before, and the smell was quite bad, but I soldiered on. I honestly thought this was a waste of time, but apparently Iggy and Jaxson didn't.

When Jaxson pushed open the door, I inhaled the warm salt air, humid though it was.

"Glinda?" said a voice from the corner.

I spun around and found Genevieve huddled on the far side. I rushed over to her. "Are you okay?"

"Yes. Or rather no. Did you know that someone killed Barbara?"

She sounded genuinely distraught, implying she had nothing to do with her host's death. "I did. The sheriff is looking for you. He really could use your input."

"Me?"

"Yes, you. You were in the knitting circle. Do you know of anyone in that group who could have done this?" I know that Fifi thought the person who'd trashed her store had been a member. And she had been right.

"How would I know?"

She wasn't going to make this easy, though it was possible she had no idea. "I don't know, but you have skills we humans don't. It will be hard, but we need to find out who killed Barbara. Who's to say he or she won't come after someone else?"

I had no basis for that comment, but I wanted Genevieve to cooperate. It wasn't as if we could force her. She'd just disappear.

"Why would anyone want to harm her?" she asked. "She didn't abandon any of them."

Ouch. That almost sounded like a confession, but it was Steve's job to get her to tell the truth. I looked at Jaxson to help me out, but he glanced to the side, indicating he had nothing. Iggy crawled out of my purse, down my leg, and went over to Genevieve.

"You need to help us. Hugo is really upset that you left."

I didn't understand the relation between those two comments, but hopefully Genevieve would do as Iggy asked.

"Okay." She stood. "The sheriff really thinks I can help?"

"Yes, he does," I said. "Penny told me about this woman who was in your knitting circle who was mad at Fifi, because she thought that her boyfriend was interested in Barbara. Do you remember her?"

"Laura Singletary."

"Yes, that's her. What did you think of her?"

"Her boyfriend is Jeffrey Godfrey. Laura was snippy. Is that the right word?" she asked.

"If you mean she wasn't overly friendly, then yes."

"When Barbara left the back room to help someone in the main store, Laura asked what we thought of Barbara."

This ought to be good. "Did you tell her that she'd kicked you out of her house when you were young?" Please say no.

"No, but I said that Barbara—or rather Fifi—could be mean at times."

That wasn't good. "How did the others respond?"

"They didn't say anything."

"Do you remember Penny? She's a good friend of mine."

"Yes. She was sweet."

I was happy that Genevieve had a good memory. "She is. Do you think you can talk to the sheriff? He'll ask you questions that might help you remember the other women."

"Okay."

One second she was there, and the next she wasn't. "Ah, did she just teleport out of here?"

Iggy spun around. "I hate when that happens."

I had to smile. "Hop in my purse. It's time to go."

"You don't have to ask me twice. Now I have to wash my feet."

"Bird poop too much for you?"

"Don't mock. If you stepped in dog poo, you would be mad, too."

I smiled. "You are right."

As soon as Penny's shift finished, we hurried out of the Tiki Hut grill and crossed the street. "What does the sheriff need to know exactly?" she asked.

I'd left Iggy with Jaxson since my familiar had a tendency to put in his two cents when we were discussing a case. "Steve thinks a good place to start is to learn who was in the knitting circle."

"He thinks one of us killed her?"

Poor Penny. "Not you, but you said you didn't know a few of the ladies. Maybe one of them had it in for Fifi."

"Maybe, but it wasn't as if we discussed killing her."

My friend was so cute. I pulled open the department's front door, enjoying how her skirt jangled and jingled with each step. I once asked her if the noise from the sewn on pennies ever bothered her, and Penny told me she'd gotten used to it.

"Hey, Pearl."

"Penny, Glinda. Nice to see you both again."

I was just there, but Penny hadn't been. "You, too."

"The sheriff is waiting for you. Go on back."

"Thanks."

As promised, Steve was at his desk. Since I expected he'd want the names of those who were at each of the two knitting classes, Penny had already drawn up a list, though she said she couldn't remember everyone.

"Have a seat ladies. Penny, I'm sorry to drag you over here right after work, but thank you for coming."

"Sure. I'm happy to help, but I don't think I know much. No one bragged about wanting to kill the new owner, you know."

Steve seemed to work hard not to smile. "I understand."

She handed him the names. "This is everyone I remember. I didn't know the last names of some of them."

"Considering you work at a restaurant, I'm surprised you didn't know them all."

"The one lady, Laura Singletary, I think her name was, was fairly new to Witch's Cove. She lives on the edge of town with her boyfriend."

Steve consulted his yellow pad. "A Jeffrey Godfrey. I was told he helped Barbara with a plumbing issue. I'll ask him to come in and tell me his side of the story."

I hoped he'd spoken to Barbara's landlord or former home owner to see if there were any existing plumbing problems. Barbara might have asked Jeffrey to help as a way to get to know him better.

"Jeffrey Godfrey isn't a suspect, is he?" I couldn't see any motivation for him wanting to kill Barbara, unless the two had messed around, and Barbara threatened to tell his girlfriend. Laura, on the other hand, might have been jealous, though even that was a bit of a stretch. I will never understand why my mind always went in a dark direction.

"Everyone is a suspect." Steve said.

"Speaking of which, did you get a hold of her ex-husband? He had stopped by the yarn shop. If he wanted to get back with his ex-wife and she turned him down, it might have upset him."

"Anything is possible. I did speak with Craig Simons over the phone to let him know about the death of his ex-wife."

"Did he seem upset?" I asked.

"I wouldn't say he was distraught, but he acted quite concerned."

"Did he admit that he'd come down to Witch's Cove to speak with Barbara?"

"Yes. He said that he was passing through town and stopped in to see how his ex-wife was doing with the shop. Before you ask, he never suggested they get together again."

"Hmm. I'll have to ask Courtney if she misunderstood."

"You do that." Steve looked between the two of us. "I'll check these names, but is there anyone else who might have wanted to harm Barbara?"

"I only met the woman after Genevieve trashed the store," I said. "Did Genevieve give you any hints when you last spoke with her?"

"No, but I think she knows something."

"Like what?" I asked.

"I don't know. She didn't tell me."

Steve was on a roll today. "What would you like Penny and me to do?"

He leaned back in his seat. "Pick Hugo's brain. If Genevieve knows anything, she'll tell him, I bet."

"I'll try, but that will require Iggy. I'm not positive my familiar will tell me something if he thinks it will harm Hugo in any way."

"Fair enough," he said. "Didn't you tell me you liked to use a white board to list all of the suspects?"

He knew about that? "Yes. Why?"

"How about having your powwow at the Hex and Bones. Bring Iggy. If Genevieve, Hugo, and Andorra are there, Genevieve might remember something."

That was actually a good idea. "I'll give it a try."

Chapter Eleven

THE WHOLE GANG was assembled in the back room of the Hex and Bones store—Jaxson, Rihanna, Iggy, Andorra, Drake, Penny, Hugo, and Genevieve. Andorra had set up a white board for me, and I was anxious to get started. Because this might be a lengthy event, I'd purchased food from the Tiki Hut Grill as a thank you for everyone pitching in to help.

"Ready?"

I felt like a middle school teacher again, only this time, the faces actually showed interest in finding out who'd killed Barbara. Not that Steve and Nash weren't competent lawmen, but I had the sense that Genevieve and Hugo might be able to help in a different way. I had no evidence that magic was involved, but our special talents might help solve the case.

"Draw your lines, Glinda," Rihanna said, understanding exactly how I worked. Clearly, she could tell I was daydreaming.

I drew two vertical lines equally spaced apart on the white board. Since this was the first time Genevieve and Hugo had seen me go through this exercise, I explained my process. "In the first column, we'll list possible suspects. In the second, a motive, and in the third, we'll give them a number from one to ten. One means this person is a long shot, and you can guess what a ten means." I looked around. "To quote our sheriff, everyone is a suspect. Who wants to go first?"

Genevieve raised her hand, which I thought was odd. Where would she have picked up that habit. I doubt she would have learned that from sitting on top of a church, which led me to believe she'd attended school with Barbara way back when. "Yes?"

"Laura Singletary. Why? Because you said Barbara picked her for vandalizing the store. Just because she was wrong about that doesn't mean Laura didn't kill Barbara."

"Excellent observation." I wrote her name on the board, reminding people that she was Jeffrey Godfrey's girlfriend. To let people know who he was, I put plumber next to his name. "And the motive?"

"She didn't want Barbara to steal her boyfriend. As much as I didn't like young Barbara, she turned out to be a beautiful woman."

"Jealousy it is. And a rating?" I looked around. I didn't want Genevieve to control everything.

"A six," Andorra said.

I had no problem with that. We could always change the designation at any time. "Anyone else?" When no one said anything, I jotted down the suggested rank. "Next?"

"What about Fifi's ex-husband?" Jaxson said.

"Why?" It didn't matter that I suspected him, too.

"Let's say for argument's sake, he was ordered to pay alimony but could no longer afford it. He might have thought if he and Barbara got back together, he wouldn't have to pay her anymore."

"Do we even know if he was paying alimony?" I looked

around, but no one responded.

"I don't," Jaxson said.

"That's okay. It's not critical at this juncture, but it could be a good motive."

"Glinda, you said that Courtney told you that Barbara wanted nothing to do with her ex-husband. If she turned him down, he might have become desperate. The only way out of his financial dilemma might have been to kill her," Jaxson said. "That's assuming the murder had to do with money and not something else."

"I like it." I wrote down Craig Simons' name. "What rank should we give him?"

"How about a four?" Drake said. "It seems pretty thin to me."

It did to me, too, but I wrote down the suggested four. I personally would have gone with a three. "Do we know if he had a girlfriend? I don't think he and Fifi had been divorced long enough for him to remarry, but I'm just guessing."

"I could find out if he has a girlfriend," Genevieve offered.

"How? I believe Craig lives up north, unless he followed Barbara down here."

"No. He didn't move. I'll go to his house and see if he is dating anyone."

I'm not sure she realized that girlfriends didn't necessarily live with their boyfriends. Jaxson and I didn't, nor did Andorra and Drake. But I let it go. "I don't have a problem with you checking it out as long as you don't—" I didn't get to finish my sentence before she'd disappeared—"talk to him."

"Did she go where I think she went?" Jaxson asked.

"I think so," I said. "Genevieve is rather impulsive."

"Hugo said that she wants to find Barbara's killer," Iggy said.

I didn't ask Andorra if that was correct since I'm sure she would have corrected him if Iggy had misunderstood Hugo. "We all want to find the killer."

I'd just finished my sentence when Genevieve returned. "He has a girlfriend. They were fighting when I got there." She held up a hand. "Don't worry. They didn't see me."

"You cloaked yourself, right?" She grinned and nodded, clearly pleased with herself. "Of course you did. Do you know what they were fighting about?"

"Barbara. But I didn't want to be gone too long, so I didn't really find out a lot."

"You were gone but a few seconds." I wonder if she wasn't able to bend the time-space continuum, like what happened when we traveled back in time?

"I really wanted to appear and tell them she was dead, but I thought your sheriff was going to call the ex-husband and tell him."

"He spoke with Craig. Are you sure the ex-husband wasn't telling his friend that Barbara was dead?" I hope she went to the right house.

"No, I'm not sure." She looked at the floor, and Hugo clasped her hand for support.

"That's okay," I said. "You did well."

I wrote down that Craig Simon had a girlfriend. Hopefully, someone would learn her identity. "I'm guessing jealousy or maybe money was the underlying issue. It's possible Craig might have given a lot of money to Barbara to help her open her store and didn't leave enough for the girlfriend. What number should we give her?"

"A five," Rihanna said. "We know nothing about her, but she has a good motive.

Jealously and greed were strong ones. "It's quite a drive from the Panhandle to Witch's Cove. It would be hard to come here, kill Barbara, and return without Craig finding out."

"Then a four."

I wrote down four point five. "Next?"

Andorra looked over at Hugo. "You'd never harm anyone, especially someone who wouldn't harm me. Okay, okay." Andorra blew out a breath. "Hugo said that to be totally fair, his name should be on the board."

That was a surprise. "Why?"

"Barbara mistreated and hurt Genevieve years ago. It would be the least he could do to protect her honor. He made sure to tell me that he didn't do it, and if he had, he certainly wouldn't have used a knitting needle."

My respect for Hugo rose dramatically. "Hugo it is. His motive is defending Genevieve's honor. His ranking?"

No one said anything. Iggy finally piped up. "He said to give him a three." I tried not to laugh as I wrote down that ranking. "If we are going to be totally fair, we should put down Genevieve, too. She trashed Barbara's place."

"I'd give her a five," Andorra said.

"But I didn't do it!"

"Hugo didn't do it either, but we're trying to look at all of the options. Don't worry; you can't be put in jail. Besides, you wouldn't have stabbed her with a knitting needle either,"

Andorra said.

"No, I would have electrocuted her. The sheriff would have thought she touched some malfunctioning power cord," Genevieve said.

"I knew it," Iggy nearly shouted. "You can control lightning."

"No, but I can harness electricity somewhat."

This was blowing my mind once more. "Do we know where on her body Barbara was stabbed?" I asked.

"Is it important?" Genevieve asked.

"It would make a difference if the person stabbed her from behind or from the front."

"Why?" Genevieve asked. "Dead is dead."

"I have little to no basis for this, but I would think a man would stab her when standing in front of her. Woman often prefer to use poison over guns. If a woman were to stab Barbara, I would think it would be from behind."

"I can ask Gavin," Rihanna said. "He already texted me and said he was back in Witch's Cove. That's earlier than he'd planned, but his mom had Barbara's body to autopsy."

"I'm glad they were only a few hours away. That would be great if he lets something slip. We can use all of the inside information we can get." I looked around. "Any other suspects?"

"What about Samuel Dickens?" Jaxson suggested.

"You think the Vice President of the Witch's Cove bank would kill someone?" I didn't know the man all that well, but I couldn't imagine he'd jeopardize his career. He could rent another space."

"Maude said he was upset that he wasn't able to rent a

space on the main avenue. If his wife's mobility isn't the best, there may not be time to wait for another storefront to become available," Jaxson said. "On second thought, is she able to run a store if moving around is difficult?"

"Where this is a will, there is a way," I said. "As far as Mr. Dickens is concerned, the man has gout," I said. "Or at least he used to."

"All the more reason to stab her from behind—assuming that was how she was killed," Jaxson said.

We were not there to argue. Everyone was a suspect. I wrote down Samuel Dickens. "I take it his motive was the love of his wife?" I asked. Jaxson nodded. "And his ranking?"

"A three," Rihanna said.

I didn't know why she picked that number, but that was okay. I wrote it down. "Anyone else?" When no one answered, I took a photo of the white board since this board belonged to Andorra. I would transfer the information to ours back at the office later. "Great. Let's eat."

THE NEXT MORNING, instead of going straight to work, I stopped at Broomsticks and Gumdrops. I wanted to learn who told Courtney about Barbara's ex-husband wanting to get back with her, especially since that wasn't what the ex-husband claimed.

The store wasn't open yet, but when I spotted Courtney inside, I tapped on the door, smiled, and waved.

Courtney grinned and opened up. "Hey. You're up early."

I stepped inside. "Tell me about it. I couldn't sleep." I

detailed our brainstorming session last night.

"You were productive. Can I help in some way?"

Courtney was smart. "I hope so. Who told you that Fifi's ex-husband wanted to get back with her but that she wasn't having any of it?"

"Hmm. I don't know her name, nor have I ever seen her before, but I haven't lived here long enough to learn everyone's name."

That was disappointing. "What did she look like?"

"She was in her thirties, I'd say. Tall, a pretty face, with long, black hair."

If there was a lineup, she might be an easy one to pick out, but no one I knew fit that bill. I wonder if she was Craig Simons' girlfriend who wanted to find out if he was cheating on her. "Did you get the sense this woman was trying to pick your brain about Fifi? She might have been tossing out an excuse to get you to talk."

Courtney's eyes opened. "Maybe. She did ask what I'd heard, but I told her the truth—that I'd only met Fifi once or twice, and that we didn't share life stories."

"Okay, thanks."

Dominic came out of the back room. "Hey, Glinda. Do you need me to help with anything?"

I had to think about that. "We have a lot of suspects. I'm not sure about some of them, but there will come a point where we might need someone to follow one of them, if you'd be up for that."

"Absolutely."

Courtney turned around and planted a hand on Dominic's chest. "Are you trying to get out of working for me?"

He grinned. "Never. I would do this on my own time." He leaned over and brushed his lips against hers. I was so happy to see them getting along so well.

I cleared my throat. "I need to be going, but Dom, I'll be in touch. And thank you, Courtney."

"Anytime. By the way, I'm quite an accomplished knitter. If the new owner keeps it a knitting store, and you need a spy, let me know."

That would let me off the hook. "You're on!"

After a quick hug and a promise the four of us would go out one night, I headed to the office. Iggy had said he'd go over on his own. That was Iggy speak for saying he just wanted to be with Jaxson, but that worked for me.

When I stepped inside, both Jaxson and my cousin, who was petting Iggy, were there. "This is a nice surprise," I said to Rihanna. "You're usually out and about by now."

Her brows rose. "I could say the same to you. You're up early."

I explained about my inability to sleep. "I stopped over at the candy store to speak with Courtney." I explained that she didn't know the woman's name who told her that Barbara's ex-husband had been in Witch's Cove to speak with Barbara. "It could have been Craig Simons' girlfriend checking up on him."

"That would make sense," Jaxson said.

Rihanna lifted her chin. "I learned something from Gavin."

I set down my purse and slipped onto the chair across from her. "Do tell."

Chapter Twelve

"Gavin said his mom turned in a preliminary autopsy report to the sheriff, so Gavin didn't feel bad telling me what she'd concluded so far."

"Tell me."

"Apparently, the knitting needle entered the right side of Fifi's neck. It was thrust upward, but the strange part was its velocity was something his mom had never seen before."

"What do you mean?" I asked.

"Gavin said he didn't want to get into the gory details, but his mom didn't have the equipment to test just how much force was used to push it in so deeply."

I had to think about that. "Does Elissa think a man committed the crime?"

"She's not saying one way or the other until there are further tests conducted—hence the preliminary part."

"Did she hint at the fact that magic might have been involved?"

Rihanna chuckled. "You do know that people can kill without using magic?"

"I know, but I don't want to rule it out."

"Why don't you ask her if you can use your magic necklace on Barbara before Gavin's mom sends off the body."

My pulse soared. "What kind of additional test does she need to have done?"

"It almost looked as if someone shot a knitting needle out of an air gun or something instead of just stabbing Barbara with it. The force was that great. The lab in Tampa should be able to tell."

"Wow. I suppose I could offer my help. If nothing comes of it, there's no harm."

"Go for it."

I thought about calling first, but I believed I had a better chance of success if I just showed up. Normally, I wouldn't have considered magic being involved if Genevieve hadn't come on the scene. After all, she had been the one to trash Fifi's Yarn Shop. While I didn't think our new gargoyle had anything to do with Barbara's death, something strange was going on with this case.

Because it was extra sticky out today, I opted to drive to the morgue, even though I would have to go home after the visit to shower so I didn't stink up the office. Sometimes, even I couldn't handle my smelly clothes.

Once at the morgue, I entered the main room. Since no one was there, I guessed that Dr. Sanchez and Gavin were in the autopsy room. Heaven forbid there had been a second murder.

As if they had a camera pointed at the entrance, the autopsy door opened, and Gavin stepped out. "Glinda, hi. Rihanna said you were stopping over. Mom is pulling out Ms. LaRue's body now."

That was what I called service. Elissa popped her head out. "You must be psychic."

I smiled. "Why is that?"

"This case is driving me crazy. I was hoping you'd lend your expertise."

"I'm happy to." Hopefully, I wouldn't disappoint her.

"Come on back. I have the body ready. Good thing Rihanna called when she did. I was getting ready to deliver her to the lab in Tampa."

"That was lucky."

I entered the autopsy room. No matter how many times I'd been back there, the stench still bothered me. It didn't matter that I acclimated quickly.

From the wound in the corpse's neck, it seemed rather obvious how she died. What I hadn't expected was the exit wound. "That was one powerful knitting needle."

"Exactly. The angle of entry seems strange to me. Heck, everything about this seems strange. You know I don't like to prejudice you, so can you just do your thing?"

"Sure." As I reached for my necklace, I sensed a quick shot of heat coming off the gem, something I don't remember happening exactly like that before. "Ouch."

"What is it, Glinda?"

"It was as if my necklace was trying to tell me something. It almost burned my skin." I rubbed the area, which was still warm to the touch.

"Has that happened before?" Elissa asked.

"Not like that. When my grandmother is trying to contact me from beyond, the gem always pulses and heats slightly—but it never has almost burned me before."

I unclasped my necklace. Even before I was able to place the gem near Barbara's feet, the stone changed from pink to yellow.

"It changed color," Elissa said. "Doesn't the yellow mean magic is involved?"

"Yes, but I'm confused why it would indicate that. The cause of death is quite obvious." Though I must not believe that completely, or I wouldn't have come over.

"I agree, but how about finishing your scan?"

"Of course." I wasn't the medical examiner. She was.

I began as usual by swinging the gem over Barbara's feet, back and forth in a slow, steady rhythm. As I moved up the body, the light yellow glow remained constant.

It was when I swung the pendant near the wound that things changed. The gem flashed a very bright yellow, along with intermittent flashes of dark blue.

"What does that color mean?" Elissa asked.

I couldn't lie. "I don't know, but I'll try to find out." I held up a finger. "Since my pendant turned really hot, I probably should ask my grandmother since it is her pendant, but that would involve a séance. From past experience, Nana doesn't show up unless it is absolutely necessary."

"Maybe we won't need her." Elissa walked around the table, and I stepped back. When presented with the possibility of magic being involved, it appeared as if Elissa was reevaluating things. "I put the time of death at around nine p.m., but maybe I need to change the time."

"Because of my pendant being hot?" I didn't want to be responsible for a wrong diagnosis.

"The heat gives me an idea. I noticed some singe marks on several of Barbara's cells. It was almost as if she'd been burned just enough to confuse the time of death."

I had to do the math. "Meaning she died earlier in the day? Like six or maybe even five?"

"I couldn't say exactly, but yes, it would have been earlier."

"The only person I know who could heat up something is now in jail." Unless it was Genevieve. She said she could have electrocuted Barbara. Yikes. I really hoped she wasn't involved in this.

"I remember hearing about that case. It happened at the bookstore, right?"

"Yes."

Elissa pulled out her phone. "I'm going to call Steve. I'm not sure if changing the time of death will affect much, but I like being accurate."

"I'm glad I could provide a different opinion." That sounded like I was bragging, but I liked it when I could help.

"You did at that. I feel more confident in my analysis. The big question was how was her body heated?"

"By magic?"

"That would be my guess, especially since your pendant turned yellow. There is nothing else that would explain it," she said. "The heated cells were so random that I can't tell how it was done."

"Could she have been electrocuted?" Maybe that was what the blue color was for.

"No, the cell pattern would be different."

I let out a slow breath of relief that Genevieve wasn't involved. I shivered at the thought that someone with that kind of magical skills was running around Witch's Cove, though.

After I said goodbye to Gavin, I headed back home to clean up. I didn't need to hear Iggy tell me that I smelled.

I'd just finished washing up and changing my clothes when my cell rang. It was probably Jaxson wondering where I was. I grabbed my phone and didn't look at the caller ID. "Hey."

"Glinda, it's Sheriff Rocker."

I stilled. Why was he being so formal all of a sudden? "Sheriff."

"Can you come over to the station? I just got off the phone with Dr. Sanchez."

Someone must have been in his office for him to be like that. "I'll be right over."

"Thank you."

He sounded so serious that I practically ran across the street. By the time I arrived, sweat had plastered my shirt to my back. So much for my refreshing shower. Thankfully, the inside of the office was cool.

"Hey, Pearl."

"Glinda. Steve is in the conference room. He asked that you go back there." Her pursed lips set my nerves on edge.

"Thanks."

Did he think I'd done something wrong by going behind his back and using my necklace on Barbara's body? It wasn't as if I hadn't done that several times in the past.

I tapped the glass and went in. "What's up?"

He shut off the video feed on the television screen. "Sorry to make my call sound so urgent, but Barbara's ex-husband is driving down from the Panhandle, and I wanted your opinion before he arrived."

Okay. I didn't expect that turn of events, but I was rather pleased he wanted to consult with me. I sat down. "What caught your attention about Dr. Sanchez's call?"

"Elissa said that Barbara's time of death might have been as much as three or four hours earlier than she first thought. No one was near the store at the time we *thought* Barbara was killed, but before that, someone did go into the store. See if you know this man, or if anything he does looks suspicious—magic wise."

"Sure. Where are the cameras?"

"One is over the door facing the street, but when the man enters, he is looking down. However, there is one camera inside. Remember, we installed them after the bookstore fire."

"I remember."

Steve played the video that showed a man I didn't recognize go inside. "Barbara is backing away, kind of implying she might know him and is afraid of him."

"I agree," he said. "I'm sorry there is no audio."

That meant I had to watch their body language. They chatted a bit, but the man never moved. The whole time his back was to the camera. Had he been to the store before? Did he know where the camera was located?

As much as I wanted to think ill of him, he didn't show any signs of aggression toward Barbara. After a minute or so, she shook her head. Had she not turned her back to the man, we might have been able to catch a few more words—assuming we had a lip reader. He didn't stay long before he left.

"That looked innocent enough," I said. "What drew your attention?"

"Keep watching."

Once outside, the man took about three steps, presumably to go to his car. He then turned around and did some odd hand waving with his right hand and then made a downward flicking motion with the other. The interior light went out, which appeared as if Barbara was ready to close. "I'm not really seeing anything. The time stamp reads 5:07 PM. She closes at five, I think."

"On the surface, it looks rather innocent, but I swear there's something there. I just can't tell what."

"Would you mind if I ask Genevieve to take a look at the film? She has talents even I don't understand."

"Do you think she might recognize the hand signals as some kind of magic spell?"

"I can't promise that, but it's possible." I personally couldn't remember seeing anyone just wave a hand and have a spell occur. That being said, I'd never seen anyone shoot fire out of their fingertips either, but that action had been caught on tape in the past.

"Then sure, call her."

I contacted Andorra and asked if Genevieve could come to the station to help—for real this time. I had just hung up when our teleporting wonder appeared at the table.

She grinned. "How can I help?"

I pressed a palm to her arm, partly to make certain she was solid, which she was. "Genevieve, we appreciate you coming so quickly, but we don't need people seeing you just pop up out of thin air."

"Oh. Sorry. I thought this was urgent."

Once more, she appeared to be rather innocent, but I

wondered if it was some kind of act? "Steve has something he wants you to watch."

"Sure."

Steve cued up the video. Genevieve said nothing during the short interaction with Barbara.

When the man drove off, Steve faced her. "What did you think?"

"I think Barbara was afraid of her ex-husband."

I stiffened. "That was Craig Simons?"

"Yes, why?"

It was Steve's place to tell her. Not mine.

"What else did you pick up?" Steve asked without losing a beat. I admired that trait in him.

"He turned off the light at the end, but I couldn't quite tell what he was trying to do with his first hand motion."

"Hold it," Steve said. "Mr. Simons was outside when the interior lights went out. How could he have turned them off?"

She lifted her chin. "Like this."

Genevieve raised her arm and flicked her fingers downward as if she was turning off some imaginary light switch. Only the lights in the conference room actually went off.

"Genevieve? You did that?" Steve asked.

"Yes." The lights came back on.

"Mr. Simons is a warlock?" I don't know why I asked. It was rather apparent. It shouldn't surprise me, especially since his ex-wife was a witch.

"He is, unless Barbara turned them off. I don't know where the light switches are located."

That put a different spin on things. The front door of the sheriff's department opened and who should walk in but none other than Mr. Simons himself. I stood. "Genevieve, we need to go, but don't disappear. It will freak out Barbara's ex-husband."

She smiled sweetly. "Okay."

"Thank you, Glinda. And Genevieve."

We both walked out together, and I made a point not to stare at Barbara's ex-husband. I couldn't say why exactly, but he was more intimidating in person, in part because the man was really tall.

Once outside, I escorted Genevieve back to the Hex and Bones shop.

"I have an idea," Genevieve said once inside.

"What is that?"

"How would you like to know what the sheriff and Barbara's ex-husband are talking about?"

"Did you plant a recording device under the table or something?" I wouldn't put anything past her.

"No, silly. I'll cloak myself and listen."

"That isn't legal."

"Oh."

I waited for her to say she wouldn't do it, but she immediately disappeared right before my eyes. Darn. I didn't have the chance to tell her not to go.

Andorra came over. "How did it go?"

"We need to talk."

"Come into the back, unless you don't want Hugo to hear. I have a feeling he'll tell Genevieve everything we discuss."

I thought about that for a moment. "That's okay."

The store had about four people inside, but Bertha would

be able to handle that number of customers. Since no one was freaking out, they must not have been looking in Genevieve's direction when she went poof.

"When is Elizabeth coming back?" Her cousin had been visiting relatives for what seemed like forever.

"Tomorrow. What with Barbara's death, we told her we could use her here. Memaw is a bit frazzled."

"Frazzled? About what? She didn't know Barbara."

"I know, but Mr. Richards showed up earlier today."

"What did the owner want?" Ever since we'd had the fundraiser that helped pay for all of the necessary upkeep on this strip of stores, he hadn't shown his face around town much.

"He's totally freaked out about Barbara's death. He told Memaw that he's thinking about selling this strip mall."

"What? Why?"

"He never wanted to be a landlord in the first place, but after his dad died, he was kind of forced into taking over."

That had to be tough. "I'm glad my parents never thought I should run a funeral home."

She smiled. "You are too well-suited to finding out who commits crimes."

I wasn't sure that was true, but I wanted to believe it. We pulled out two chairs in the back room and sat down. "You'll never guess who showed up to the yarn shop shortly before Barbara was murdered," I said.

"Who?"

"Her ex-husband, Craig Simons."

Andorra whistled. "What did he want, do you suppose?"

I relayed what Courtney had heard. "After looking at the

video of their interaction, I have to say Barbara didn't look happy that he was there. Her ex is with the sheriff right now, and if I had to guess, Genevieve is too, ready to get the scoop."

Andorra planted both palms on her face. "She can't be doing that."

"I know. I told her. Any idea how to stop her?"

"Good luck." Andorra looked over at Hugo, listened for a moment, and then turned back to me. "Hugo said he'll speak with her."

"After the fact." To be honest, I couldn't wait to hear what Craig Simons told the sheriff.

"Yes, after the fact." Andorra's brows rose, understanding that I would be asking Genevieve to spill the beans.

Chapter Thirteen

IT WAS A good thirty-minutes before Genevieve popped up in the back room of the Hex and Bones. "That ex-husband is a piece of work," she said.

Where did a stone statue pick up such an idiom? Right now though, her education wasn't my concern. Even though what Genevieve did wasn't legal, I couldn't help but ask what she knew. "Tell me."

She opened up two more of the folding chairs and then motioned for Hugo to join her. I thought it cute that she wanted to be near him. "Craig Simons admitted that his real purpose for visiting Barbara was to warn her about some guy by the name of Norman Eastwick. It wasn't to see how Barbara was coming along with the store. Apparently, that's what he told the sheriff over the phone."

I wonder why he didn't tell the truth the first time? "Are we supposed to know this Norman Eastwick?" I asked.

"I don't know, but according to Craig, this Norman guy came to Craig's house, because he didn't know Barbara and Craig had divorced. Norman said he really needed to talk with her."

"Why did Norman Eastwick want to talk to her?" I asked.

"Here's the good part. About six months ago—though it

could have been longer, I can't remember since I'm not great with dates—Norman was under the influence and crashed into Barbara's car."

"Was anyone hurt?" Andorra asked with concern.

"Only the cars. Apparently, the repairs were going to be extensive, and naturally Barbara wanted Norman to pay for it."

"Let me guess," I said. "Norman didn't have insurance."

She shrugged. "I don't know, but he told her that if he got one more DUI—whatever that meant—he would be fined or thrown into jail. He begged her not to tell the cops. He promised to pay her two thousand dollars a month until he'd paid for the repairs."

"That sounds like a good honest thing to do—pay that is. Asking her to keep it from the cops is criminal, however," I said. "I sense there is more."

"Yes. Norman paid Barbara the full six payments. He thought all was well until she demanded another five thousand dollars."

I whistled. "I'm guessing that the ex-husband will claim he knew nothing about this, right?" I asked.

"He knew she'd been in a wreck, but she told him the other person's insurance would pay. He wasn't happy with Barbara's deception."

I shook my head. "I knew it."

"What?" Andorra asked.

"The first time I met Fifi, or rather Barbara, I didn't know who she really was. When I asked her who might have trashed her store, she mentioned Laura Singletary, the plumber's girlfriend. After we discussed it a bit more, Rihanna asked if perhaps someone was blackmailing her, and if this could be the person's way of showing her that he or she was serious."

Andorra's mouth opened wide and then closed. "Rihanna must be psychic. Except in this case, she got it backward."

"I know, but blackmail was involved. Money might be the motive in this murder, not jealousy."

Andorra shrugged. "True. Norman might have thought she'd never stop demanding he pay, which was what motivated him to kill her. Anything else, Genevieve?"

"No."

"That's great intel. Thank you. If we can believe the ex-husband, Norman sounds like the guilty party. How did the sheriff react to what Craig told him?" I asked.

Genevieve sighed. "It was difficult to tell. Your Steve Rocker is a hard one to get a good read on."

"He certainly can be. Did this Norman guy ask the ex-husband where to find Barbara?" I asked.

"Yes, but according to Craig, he refused to tell him where she'd moved to. Craig didn't think he'd been followed when he drove down here, but considering Barbara is dead, maybe he was."

"I wonder what Norman does for a living? It takes skill to tail someone and not be seen." I personally hadn't developed that talent.

"I don't know, but Craig thinks that after he stopped in to see his ex-wife, Norman must have snuck in and killed her. He mentioned that a few times."

Hmm. "That sounds like he either believes Norman is the killer or he is trying to point the finger at someone beside himself. I didn't watch the video past the point of when Craig left the store to see if someone else showed up, but if Norman is our killer, then he must be a warlock. Whoever got inside without being seen had to have been able to teleport or open doors with his mind."

Genevieve shrugged. "Maybe."

"You have no idea what the ex-husband's first hand signal meant?" She said she didn't have any idea, but maybe she had time to think about it.

"No."

"Any guesses?" Andorra asked.

Genevieve scratched her chin, and then looked over at Hugo. "Oh, go ahead."

Hugo stood, acting as if he was about to put on a performance slowly lifted his arms into the air. I was about to ask what he was doing until a book on the counter rose in the air. He looked over at Genevieve, winked, and then lowered his arms. The book returned to its place.

I wasn't sure which surprised me more: the levitation or the wink. The latter seemed a bit out of character, but we had bigger things to worry about right now.

"That is very impressive, Hugo. Thank you. Genevieve, are you saying you think that the ex-husband was levitating something? Like a knitting needle maybe?"

"He could have been. You should know that no two magical entities use the same movements, but I don't know why. For all we know, he could have been waving goodbye."

She was right, but even if we knew what he was doing, no court would believe magic was used. "Steve showed me the inside camera, but I wonder what happened a few seconds after the ex-left? Let me call and ask him."

Once Steve answered, I explained that I'd watched Hugo move an object just by raising his arms. I certainly didn't tell him that Genevieve had spied on Steve. "What happened once Craig finished with the weird hand movements?"

"After he drove away, you mean?" Steve asked.

"Yes."

"Before Craig even pulled open the car door, Barbara stepped out of view of the camera. From the direction she was headed, it was to the back room. I never saw anyone else enter the shop or see someone kill her if that's what you're asking."

I figure that much. "Thanks. I was just wondering."

"Glinda?" he asked. "What are you thinking?"

"Nothing yet. When I have a more solid theory, I'll be sure to pass it by you."

"I'd appreciate it."

I disconnected. We were back to step one. "Too bad I couldn't ask Steve if he planned to bring in Norman Eastwick to confirm Craig's story."

"Why not?" Genevieve asked.

"Because he'd want to know how I learned about Norman."

"Oh."

I felt a bit sorry for her, but Steve had enough to deal with having his snoopy grandmother work in the same office. If he thought Genevieve could be at the department at any time without being seen—or in his house for that matter—he'd be rather upset.

"Anyone have any ideas how we should proceed? If the guilty party used magic to kill Barbara, we're the only ones who can catch this person," I said.

"Who are you leaning toward for the murder?" Andorra asked.

"That is an excellent question. I'm not really sure. I could say that the ex-husband did it because he was possibly able to turn off the interior lights, but what would be his motive for wanting Barbara dead? Alimony aside, they were already divorced, so he was free to be with someone else."

Andorra's brows rose. "We can't ignore the ex-husband's new girlfriend."

"No, we can't. Craig could have told her that he was planning to speak with Barbara. When he saw her, maybe he realized his mistake and wanted to get back together with her. He might have told his girlfriend it was over. The possible rejection might have been enough to kill Barbara, assuming the girlfriend was that unstable."

"Good thought. Did Steve say whether Craig was paying her alimony?" Andorra asked.

"No, he didn't say." I turned to Genevieve. "Did you learn this girlfriend's name when you were at the ex-husband's house? I know you were only there for a few seconds so maybe her name wasn't mentioned."

"Uhm. I think Bat."

"Bat? What kind of name is that?" I asked.

"Maybe he called her Matt, or Nat. Or it could have been Pat."

I worked hard not to roll my eyes. "I'll ask Steve. He's very thorough. I imagine he's looked into it."

"Can Steve get Craig's financials to see what kind of hardship it would have been to pay alimony—assuming he was paying?" Andorra asked.

"Not without cause, I don't think. Steve has no evidence that Craig is guilty of anything. It doesn't matter if Steve believes in magic or not. The courts don't."

"Darn." Andorra huffed. "What about doing a séance? I never met Barbara Lipton Simons but maybe she'd be willing to tell us something."

"That's a good idea, but those who've recently passed are often too traumatized to communicate. It doesn't hurt us to try, though. My mom is pretty good at speaking to the dead, too."

"Great. Let me know if you need me or Elizabeth to help. My cousin should be back soon."

Genevieve raised her hand. I think she must have gone to school at some point. "I can help," she offered.

"Help with what? The séance?"

"Yes."

The problem with that was that Barbara might not want to speak if Genevieve was nearby. It was Barbara who'd basically kicked out a twelve-year-old girl. As an adult, Barbara might have felt guilty. Since the conversation was beginning to become a bit uncomfortable, I stood. "I'll be in touch about that. Keep your ears to the ground, people."

I'm betting that Pearl would have wormed some information out of her grandson about this case and told her friends by now. Dinner at my aunt's restaurant might be in order.

As I approached our office, Jaxson was on the steps with a scrub brush and a bucket in hand, washing the handrail that led up to our office. "What are you doing?" I asked.

"Our resident iguana is hopping mad that his nemesis,

Tippy, has struck again." He nodded to some of the white blotches on the wood where Jaxson hadn't washed yet.

"Seriously? I mean, it's not a pleasant visual, but we live on the beach. Seagulls are a part of life."

"Tell that to Iggy. He thinks Tippy is out to get him."

I laughed. "Out to get him? Why? Did Iggy do something to upset the seagull population?"

"Ask him. Personally, he believes that when he trash talked the seagulls about the mess on top of the church, the birds heard him, and they are now taking revenge against him."

"Is that so? Wow. I hope that's not true, or I might have to wear a scarf on my head for the rest of my life. Do you need help with this?" I asked.

"Nah. I'm almost done."

"Then I'll go check on His Majesty."

I stepped around Jaxson and went inside.

"Did you see him?" Iggy asked.

"Who?"

"Tippy."

What was up with this fixation with a seagull? "Did he poop on you or something?"

"I'm not giving him the chance. I've got eyes on top of my head, you know."

No, he didn't. "Good for you."

As I went to the kitchen to grab some tea, I decided we had nothing to lose in contacting Barbara. I didn't fully understand this crossing over stuff, but if I were Fifi LaRue, or in this case Barbara Lipton Simons, I might come back to my store for closure—assuming dead people needed it.

The big question was whether Steve would let us do our séance magic in there since it might still be considered a crime scene. Of course, I could invite him or his grandmother if he was worried about us messing with the evidence, but I was sure he wouldn't participate.

Before I lost my nerve, I called him. "Glinda. Did you figure something out?"

"Not yet, which is why I wanted to see if maybe I could hold a séance at Fifi's shop, assuming you've finished processing the scene. She might be more agreeable to showing up there."

"A séance, huh? As in contacting the dead?"

I didn't know why he pretended he didn't know what a séance was. He was aware of the other ones we'd held, including the one his grandmother had participated in. "Yes. We're hoping Barbara will give us a lead."

"Oh. Okay, but can you wait an hour?"

It would take me that long to gather the troops. "Of course, but why the delay?"

"I'm over at the store now checking out the area."

"Oh. Did you find some evidence?" I wanted to keep the conversation going in the hopes that Steve would tell me about his meeting with Barbara's ex-husband.

"I'm not sure. Considering where her body was located, someone could have come in the back way."

"That's great. We have cameras back there."

He let out a loud exhale. "We did. Someone disabled them."

"How?"

"That's what I am here to find out. I can't see any evidence of tampering. They just stopped working."

"Would you like me to ask Jaxson to speak with the man who installed them to see what he thinks?" Not that I didn't believe Steve wasn't smart, but electronics might not be his forte.

"I've got it covered. But thanks."

End of that discussion. "So, we can come over in an hour then?"

"Yes. Stop by. I'll be here to let you in."

"Thanks."

Rihanna came out of her room. "Was that Steve?"

"Yes. I need to fill you and Jaxson in on my day."

Jaxson came inside with his bucket and brush. "Your highness, the handrails are now clean."

"Thank you! If I see that seagull again, I'll…"

"You'll what?" While Iggy had many talents, the ability to harm a bird wasn't one of them.

"I don't know."

I didn't want to give Iggy a chance to figure something out, so I changed the subject. "I have some interesting news about the case."

"Let me clean up, and you can tell me all about it," Jaxson said as he set the cleaning supplies by the front door.

I called Andorra while Jaxson showered. She said Elizabeth had just returned and would be happy to join us for the séance.

"Great. I'll meet you and Elizabeth at the yarn shop in fifty minutes."

"See you there."

Once Jaxson came out of the bathroom, all clean, I told

him, Iggy, and Rihanna about what Genevieve had learned. "As you've probably heard, we are doing a séance."

"I want to come," Iggy said.

I often wondered if his magic helped us contact the dead. "I'd love to have you. Rihanna?"

"I'm game."

When my hour of waiting was up, I stood. "Let's go."

Jaxson, I knew, would want to stay behind.

Chapter Fourteen

"I THOUGHT YOU needed a table and candles," Steve said as he let us into the yarn shop.

"We'll sit on the floor." I patted my purse. "I have candles in here."

"Please don't burn the place down."

"We're witches. I'm sure we can put out a fire." That was a total lie. Now, if Hugo had been with us, we wouldn't have had a problem. He possessed the ability to extinguish flames—more or less.

"Drop the key off when you are finished," he said.

"Will do."

Elizabeth, as well as Andorra, Iggy, and Rihanna were with me to do the séance. I know that Genevieve wanted to come, but like I said, I didn't think that was a good idea. Barbara might not come out to play if she sensed her nemesis was there to possibly attack her. I realize that Barbara had passed, but she might not be aware of it yet.

"Let's sit in the back," I said. "That's where Penny said Fifi held her knitting circle. Barbara might feel more comfortable surrounded by knitters. Not only that, the vibes from having her showroom messed up, and then having her ex-husband return to give her grief, might make her want to avoid that area."

"But someone murdered her back there, right?" Andorra asked.

"Yes, but let's give it a try anyway. If we fail, we fail."

They all nodded. I placed the candles in the center of the room, and we all sat on the floor, with Iggy between me and Rihanna. After I lit the candles, we all touched our fingers to the person's or animal's hand next to ours. We then closed our eyes in order to rid our minds of exterior distractions. The sulfur scent entered my nose and actually helped calm me. I now wished I'd thought to turn on the air conditioner as it was very muggy back here, but if I stood and turned it on, that would ruin everything.

It was time. "Barbara Lipton Simons. I am truly sorry for what happened to you. Please know that we are here to help you find the person who did this to you." I inhaled and then forced the tension out of my shoulders. "I wish we had spent more time together, but that did not happen. However, we need your help now to solve this terrible crime. Do you know who murdered you?"

I sucked in a breath and stilled. This was always the hardest part—waiting. Iggy wiggled, implying he, too, was impatient. I could always count on him not to follow the rules and open his eyes if he sensed a ghost. As I've instructed him to do in the past, he was to tap my hand if he saw one.

"I don't know," came the faintest of voices. I waited for the hand tap, but it never came.

"Did your ex-husband show up just to tell you about the man who hit your car?"

"Huh?" I could barely hear her.

"Was it Norman Eastwick?" I said louder.

"Yes."

Did that mean Norman Eastwick killed her or that Norman Eastwick had hit her car. I needed to be clearer. "Did Norman stab you with a knitting needle?"

The room was almost completely silent when I asked that question. If flickering candles could make a sound, they would be the only things in the room that did. My impatience gave out. I had to look. The candles had gone out and I saw no one. I lifted my hands. "She's gone."

Andorra, Elizabeth, and Rihanna all opened their eyes. I wanted one of them to say they heard something that I didn't, but they remained silent.

"What did she really say?" Elizabeth asked. "I know I've been out of town for a bit, but this woman made little sense."

"That's the problem. She didn't directly answer my question. It could have been Norman Eastwick who killed her, or maybe it wasn't. For what it's worth, she didn't come out and say he was innocent."

"Where does that leave us?" Andorra asked.

"I think she was saying that her ex-husband came to discuss Norman Eastwick," Rihanna said. "That would match what her ex-husband told the sheriff."

"True." I looked over at Iggy. Sometimes, his excellent hearing picked up things that our ears couldn't. Barbara had spoken softly. "What did you think?"

"I don't think her ex-husband killed her, or she would have said so."

"Good to know." Though that sounded like a guess to me. "What about Norman, the man who ran into her and who was paying her off every month? Do you think he had anything to do with her death?" Why Iggy would know more than we did, I don't know.

"He could be guilty if it's true that Ms. LaRue was trying to get more money from him," Iggy said.

"I have to say, Norman has a good motive for wanting Barbara dead. Maybe Steve can ask him to come in. In the meantime, our sheriff might be able to get a copy of Norman's bank statements to confirm what the ex-husband said was true." I looked at the others to see their reaction.

"I like it," Andorra said.

"Okay, I'll suggest it to him."

I mentally pictured where Barbara might have been standing based on a few of Steve's comments. He hadn't exactly been forthcoming with the details about where she'd died, just that she was walking toward the back when it happened. Since the place was carpeted, I guess he hadn't wanted to draw a chalk outline of the body. That or it explained why he'd returned—to clean up.

When I looked around, I spotted a vase of knitting needles near where Barbara's body was most likely found.

"What are you thinking?" Rihanna asked.

She probably knew, but she wanted me to state it for the sake of the others. "It's possible that Barbara doesn't know who killed her if a warlock or witch was involved."

"How so?" Elizabeth asked.

"If her back was to the front of the store, a person of magic could have swiped a hand and used telekinesis to lift the needle from that vase full of needles over there, straight into her." The angle looked like it might match.

"Eww, that's gruesome," Elizabeth said.

"I know. Even if the autopsy report states the angle of the entry wound matches the angle of a needle in the vase, that doesn't narrow down our field of suspects."

"Yes, it does. It proves that the killer has magical abilities. All we need to do is test to see who is one," Iggy said.

I picked him up. We'd run up against this problem many times before. "And how do you propose to do that?"

"We could have Genevieve or Hugo cloak themselves and follow our suspects around to see if they are witches or warlocks. Or we can do the same thing I did last time."

"Which is sneak up behind a person and yell at them to see if they can hear you?" I asked.

"Yes."

"Iggy has a point," Andorra said, "but too many of our suspects don't live in town. We might have to use Genevieve."

She could get from here to probably anywhere in seconds. I needed to pick her brain regarding her limits. "How long can she remain cloaked? Is it hours or days? I know she and Hugo don't need to sleep or eat, but what if she suddenly appears?"

Andorra shrugged. "What could the person do other than question who she was and ask her what she was doing in his or her house?"

"You're right." We did have a lot of options. "Let me return the key to Steve and discuss this with him. He might have some ideas. How about if you and Elizabeth brainstorm with Genevieve and Hugo on how to determine if a person has magic? Rihanna, Iggy, and I will stop over afterward."

"Sounds good," Elizabeth said.

After cleaning up the knitting room, we headed to the sheriff's office. I had such high hopes that the séance would be the key, but it hadn't been.

"Hey, Pearl." I held up the key to the yarn shop. "I'm returning this to Steve. May we go back?"

"How was the séance?"

Was nothing sacred? "Kind of a bust, but she did appear."

"Oh, really? Did she point a finger?"

I huffed out a laugh. "I wish."

From the way Pearl was leaning forward, she wanted me to give her more details, but I wasn't sure what those details would be. Instead of explaining, I smiled and headed back to Steve's office with Rihanna right behind me.

I knocked and entered. "I returned the key to Pearl."

"Thank you. Have a seat."

Once we were seated, Iggy crawled out of my purse, though I wasn't sure why. It was possible it was hard to breath in there, though that hadn't been an issue in the past. I'm betting he wanted to be part of the investigation.

It would be nice if he could communicate with Steve. If he was willing, I could attempt to put a spell on our sheriff like I did with Jaxson so that he could understand Iggy. It would certainly make things easier.

"We were able to contact Barbara, but I don't think she knew all that much."

Steve looked like he was fighting a smile. "What did she say?"

Rihanna and I, with some help from Iggy, told him what we remembered. "My question about Norman was poorly worded. She told us that she didn't know who murdered her.

If I can take a little liberty with her words, Norman Eastwick also came to Craig Simons to discuss the possible blackmail."

He nodded. "That aligns with what Craig told us."

That gave me my lead. "Do you plan on bringing Norman Eastwick in?"

His brows rose. "I probably will." Steve studied me. "You're planning something. I can tell."

I huffed out a breath. I hadn't even mentioned my idea to anyone yet. "The key is to first figure out whether someone has magical abilities. If not, they probably aren't the killer."

"We've been through this before. Are you going to have Iggy shout at them from his cloaked form to see if they respond?"

Iggy looked up at me. "Let me, let me."

"Maybe. As I see it, we have a few suspects, some with a better motive than others. We can start with them."

He pulled out his yellow pad from his desk drawer. "Go through them again."

"Fine. My top suspect—assuming he has magical talents—is this new entry, Norman Eastwick. If Barbara was blackmailing him, he might take things into his own hands."

"Hold it. How did you learn about Norman Eastwick again?" he asked. "I never mentioned his name."

Uh-oh. I couldn't tell him that Genevieve told me. "Barbara's ghost told us."

The raised brows implied he didn't completely believe me, but most likely he had no idea how else I could have learned about it.

"I see. To fill you in, I already have a call into the judge to see if we can look at his financials. I'll also ask if I can look at

Barbara's. It should show the payments from Norman Eastwick for the car."

I was impressed that Steve was one step ahead of me. "Great job. My second choice is the ex-husband."

"Why? They were already divorced."

I shrugged. "Could be any one of many reasons. He could have wanted to get back with her. She might have mocked him, saying all sorts of insulting things. Or, he could have told her he couldn't afford the alimony anymore—assuming he was paying in the first place—and she told him to leave."

He nodded and jotted down the information. "Interesting."

"It would be more so if the ex-husband is a warlock."

"Do you have proof he killed her other than those fancy hand signals?"

"No."

I listed the other possible subjects and their motives. "I know nothing about Craig's girlfriend, though. I don't even know her name."

He flipped to another page in his pad. "Natalie Gibson."

That aligned with what Genevieve thought. "Good. The plumber's girlfriend is a possibility, too, but even if her boyfriend had an affair with Barbara one time, does that warrant murder?"

He dipped his chin. "I've heard a lot of crazy reasons for murder. Nothing would surprise me."

"I guess I would be remiss if I didn't mention Sam Dickens."

Steve flipped through his pages once more. "Who?"

Steve had lived here a year. He should know who that

was. "The vice president of the bank." I told him about how upset he was that he wasn't able to rent the space from Heath Richards.

"That's a stretch."

"I know."

Someone knocked on his door, and then Pearl peeked her head in. "Sorry to interrupt, but Donna, over at the Water's Edge Motel, said she just heard something about Fifi LaRue's death."

"What about it?" her grandson asked.

"A man was asking about where to find a Barbara Simons. Naturally, Donna had no idea who that was, but then the man—presumably, Norman Eastwick—described her. Donna told him that another man had also stayed there the day before and was in Witch's Cove to see Fifi LaRue, but Donna was convinced they were the same woman."

Steve's brows furrowed. "Gram, I have no idea what that means."

"I just told you. Norman Eastwick came to Witch's Cove to find Barbara. I bet he killed her."

Steve held up his hands in a T for timeout. "How did you know anything about Norman Eastwick?"

She smiled. "Walls have ears."

"Not these walls. I was in the soundproof, glass enclosed room."

She grinned. "Oh."

Before he could question her further, she slipped out.

My head was spinning. I looked over at Rihanna. "You pick up on anything?"

"My lips are sealed."

Genevieve!

Chapter Fifteen

"I HAVE AN idea," I said. "It involves Genevieve."

"What about her?" Steve asked.

"Give me a sec and I'll tell you." I called Andorra and asked if Genevieve could come over to the sheriff's office. "I'm assuming she's there?" I asked.

"She is. I don't have any idea what she and Hugo can talk about for so long, but they seem to be enjoying themselves."

"I'm sorry to interrupt their date, but this is important."

"Of course."

I swear I hadn't even swiped the phone off before Genevieve appeared.

"You rang!" Genevieve grinned.

"You can't just appear like that. What if someone else was in the office?" She seemed unable to learn.

She looked around. "But no one is."

It was no use arguing with her. "We need your help."

She grinned. "What is it you need me to do?"

I turned to Steve. "I know this might be tricky, and maybe a little unorthodox, but if you could arrest—I mean pretend to arrest—Norman Eastwick for Barbara's murder and put him in the cell, we can see if he is a warlock."

He stared at me for a moment. "Assuming I would do

that, how does arresting him prove anything?"

I turned to Genevieve. "Do you think you can do a little experiment for us?"

"If I can."

"Here's my plan. Steve will hang a set of jail keys on a hook out of reach of the cells. Once Norman is in the cell, if he is our guy, he'll use telekinesis to grab the keys, open the door, and sneak out." I turned to Steve. "You can ask Pearl to go for a cup of coffee or something, so he'll think the coast is clear. When he sneaks outside, you will be there waiting for him."

"And if he doesn't sneak out?"

"Then he might not be our man. Tell him you made a mistake and let him go."

"He could sue for false arrest. And he'd win," Steve said.

I shook my head. "If he tries, you could say that you'll tell the cops in his hometown about his DUI."

His brows scrunched. "How did you know about that?"

Uh-oh. "I heard it somewhere. I think Barbara told us."

"If she was that chatty, she should have told you who killed her."

Whoops. Think. "I'm betting her back was to the killer at the time." I hope he bought it.

He harrumphed. "Suppose I agree to this crazy idea, what role does Genevieve play?"

"I thought Genevieve could do a trial run to see if she can lift the keys from the hook and grab them." I looked over at her. Just because Hugo would have no problem with it didn't mean she'd be successful.

"I'll try."

Steve pushed back his chair. "I'm not sure about this at all, but I am curious to see Genevieve in action besides just disappearing and appearing all the time."

We went down the hallway to the cells that were thankfully empty.

Iggy had insisted on coming with us, but when he lifted his head and sniffed, I bet he regretted joining us. "This place stinks."

"Shh."

"Tell Steve he should hire a cleaning service."

"I don't think this place is meant to be a five-star hotel experience."

Steve looked over at us and smiled. I guess he didn't need to hear Iggy to understand what he'd said.

Steve placed the keys on a hook. Before I could ask Genevieve to step into the cell, she did it herself and closed the door. "Eww. You expect people to stay here?" She looked around. "The mattress is lumpy and dirty."

"It's supposed to be a deterrent," he said.

I don't know what she was complaining about. "You stayed on top of a church roof for years, subject to winds, rain, and brutal sun." And probably bird poop. "Is that any better?"

"That was different. The air was always fresh, and I occasionally left at night to do my thing." She flashed us a smile.

I didn't ask what her *thing* was. "Back to business. Can you get the keys and open the cell like a fairly normal magical person could?" Not that I'd met anyone beside Hugo who could easily move objects with his mind, but she didn't need to know that.

"Give me a sec."

Steve, Rihanna, and I stood off to the side, while Iggy peeked his head out of my purse once more. Genevieve stuck her hands out through the bars and did some kind of finger waving motion. When the keys moved, Steve's eyes widened.

It took about ten seconds before Genevieve was able to lift them off the hook. The problem was that they immediately dropped to the ground.

"Hold on. I can do this, though it might take less time to mentally open the lock."

I liked her attitude. "You may have that ability, but others might not."

"I know. That's why I'm only using telekinesis."

She did more finger moving and hand waving until she was able to send them in her direction. Once within reach, she grabbed them and opened the door. With the keys high in the air, she stepped out of the cell and grinned. "I did it."

Rihanna clapped. "Yes, you did."

"Good job." Steve slipped the keys from her fingers. "Let's see if Norman Eastwick will be as successful."

We all returned to Steve's office, but we didn't sit down. Steve had a few decisions to make regarding whether he was even going to participate in this scheme. "Let us know what you decide to do," I said.

"I will. And don't worry. I will speak with Mr. Eastwick."

"Thank you."

I made sure Iggy was secured in my bag and was about to leave when Genevieve grabbed my hand and Rihanna's. A second later we were in the back room of the Hex and Bones.

My heart dropped to my stomach. I'd time traveled a few times to understand what had happened, but this took me by surprise. "Did you just teleport us here?" Duh. Of course she did. "Why?"

"You looked like you were ready to leave."

She had to be kidding. "You can't just move people without asking first."

Genevieve looked crestfallen. "Oh, no. Was it painful?"

"No, but what will Pearl think when we don't walk out of Steve's office in a moment?"

She clamped a hand over her mouth. "I didn't think of that."

Genevieve didn't think of a lot of things. "Can you take us back? Please."

"Why?"

I inhaled to gain some patience. "So we can walk out of Steve's office like we're expected to."

She smiled. "Oh. Sure."

She clasped our hands, and instantly we were back in Steve's office. He looked up. "Where did you go?"

I turned to Genevieve. "Thank you. You can return."

"Okay."

Once she was gone, I explained how Genevieve was just trying to help when she teleported us to Hex and Bones. "I told her not to do that again. She lacks certain social awareness, shall we say."

"I see. By the way, I just spoke with Norman Eastwick. He was already on his way back to the Panhandle, but he said he'd turn around and come back here. He wants to help. I will let you know how it goes."

I mentally pumped a fist. "Thank you."

Before anything else happened, Rihanna, Iggy, and I left.

I turned to my cousin. "You haven't said much."

"I'm just thinking. While I like that Steve is going to see if Norman is a warlock, we should figure out how we are going to test the others."

"Good point. Mind if I peek in the yarn shop first?" I asked.

"Why?"

"My necklace heated for a moment." I really needed to ask Gertrude or my mom what the blue color meant."

She smiled. "It's hot outside, or are you thinking it's Nana trying to tell you something?"

"I'm not sure, but we're almost there."

She shrugged. "Okay."

"Afterward, I want to call Heath to see what he plans to do about the now open space. He'll probably have to return the five months of rent money Barbara paid to her family—whoever they are."

"If that's the case, I would imagine he'd rent it as soon as possible."

"Agreed, but that might be hard considering someone was recently murdered in this shop. That often gives people the creeps, you know," I said.

"I don't think the fact that Barbara happened to rent this space had anything to do with her murder. It's not like it's going to be haunted. People die all the time in houses and the homes still sell."

I smiled. "I hope you are right."

At the yarn shop, I peered in through the storefront window. Rihanna grabbed my arm. "I think someone's in the back. I see a light."

I looked inside. "I don't see anyone in there."

Iggy poked his head out. "Let me take a look."

He had excellent eyesight and hearing. "Sure."

I placed him against the window and then waited.

"Yes. I hear someone moving about."

"I'm calling Steve." It was possible it was Heath Richards come to see what needed to be done. "Hey, Steve."

"Did you forget something?"

"No, but there is someone inside the yarn shop. I thought you should know."

"That's probably Zelda Dickens. Heath Richards called a while ago and asked if she could check out the place. She's interested in renting the space."

That was fast. Almost too fast. "Oh. Great. I know she really wanted it."

"Anything else?"

"Not that I can think of. Later." Good thing Zelda didn't show up in the middle of the séance. Most likely Steve told Heath Richards to give us some time. I disconnected. "Let's head back to the office."

We probably should check in with Andorra again like I'd promised, but Genevieve could fill her in. If they had a good plan to tell who had magical powers and who didn't, Andorra would let me know.

When we arrived at the office, Jaxson was inside. He looked up from his desk. "How did it go?"

"It was highly interesting. Let me get a drink, and I'll fill you in."

I placed my bag on the table, and Iggy crawled out. Once I poured tea for myself and Rihanna, I returned to the main room.

"Rihanna was telling me the séance wasn't the success you were hoping for?"

"No, but Barbara did show up. That's something. I believe she confirmed that the man who had crashed into her car was Norman Eastwick. Steve has asked him to come in." I told him about our plan to test whether he is a warlock or not.

"Good luck."

He didn't sound enthusiastic. "Do you have another idea?"

"Not really, but Iggy here is pretty good at discovering if a person has any abilities."

"True. If the telekinesis trick fails, we'll let Iggy do his thing."

"Have we completely discounted the plumber and his girlfriend?" Rihanna asked.

"No one should be discounted. Maybe we can ask Genevieve to spy on them, illegal though that is."

"I'm sure she'd be happy to oblige. She's never mentioned having any difficulty staying cloaked."

"You said that Zelda is at the store now?" Jaxson asked.

"Yes, but I have no way of knowing how long she'll be there."

"I have an idea," he said.

I loved it when Jaxson participated in the planning. "Tell me."

"How about I call Dom and ask if he wants to do a little surveillance on Zelda? The quicker we can eliminate someone the better."

"I agree. What do you hope to accomplish by merely

spying on her?" I asked.

"You said we need to test all subjects to see if they have magical powers."

"We do."

Jaxson looked over at Iggy. "I know he hates being on a leash, but what if Dom walks Iggy and accidentally on purpose runs into Zelda—metaphorically not literally. You know how everyone likes to stop and ask about our cute familiar."

"True."

"If Zelda sees them, I bet she'll stop and ask what Dom, instead of you, is doing with Iggy, assuming she knows Iggy is usually with you."

I looked over at my iguana. "Do you think she knows who you are?"

He puffed out his chest. "Everyone knows me."

Oh, boy. "Give Dom a call. If Zelda is not at the store, she might be at the bank. Last I heard, she worked there, but maybe she doesn't any longer considering her health issues." I turned to Iggy. "You're good with this?"

"Yes. I'm a team player."

"Yes, you are. I will call Andorra and see if Genevieve is up for more surveillance on the plumber and his girlfriend."

"What can I do?" Rihanna asked.

"At the moment, I'm not sure. Too many of the suspects live several hours away, but once we narrow down the field, I'm sure we can keep you and your camera busy."

She smiled. "I like it."

Jaxson pulled out his phone and called Dom, while I contacted Andorra. It didn't take long to explain what I would like to have Genevieve do.

"I'll ask her, but I'm sure she'll agree. Is her only job to see if they have any powers?"

"Yes, though I'm not sure how she can accomplish that other than observing them."

"I'll tell her. I imagine we'll know something by this evening."

"Thanks." I turned to Jaxson. "Is Dom game?"

"In just a few seconds, we should hear his knock to pick up Iggy."

I stood. "I need to get his leash."

He bobbed his head. "I don't need a stinking leash."

"I know, but if you're wearing one, it will look more legit that you are being supervised."

He made some sound that I don't remember hearing before, but I bet it wasn't one of joy. "The leash is at my apartment. I'll be back in a sec."

"I can run over there," Rihanna said. "It will give me something to do."

"If you want." I fished out my keys and handed them to her. "The leash is in the kitchen drawer next to where I keep the silverware." She looked at me with a scrunched up face. "Don't judge," I shot back.

She chuckled and then left.

I turned to Jaxson. "What are the chances this works?"

"We'll soon find out."

Chapter Sixteen

No sooner had Rihanna returned with Iggy's leash than Dom came to pick him up.

"Don't worry about Iggy. If he gets tired, I'll carry him," Dom said.

"Don't spoil him too much. And don't believe everything he tells you. Iggy has a lot more stamina than he'll let on."

"Spoil sport," Iggy said.

"You know it's true. You like to see just how much you can get away with." I placed the leash around Iggy's middle. He wiggled at first but then settled down. "Dom, the bank closes shortly. If you don't find Zelda at the yarn shop or at the bank, don't worry about it. I'm sure we can try again tomorrow."

"Yes, ma'am."

Ma'am? That made me sound old. I turned to Iggy. "Be good."

"You don't have to worry about me."

"I know." In a pinch, Iggy always came through.

Once they left, I settled back on the sofa. "We have Zelda taken care of with Iggy. Genevieve will scope out Laura Singletary, and Steve will test Norman's ability to get out of the jail. That leaves us with the one other prime candidate—

that of the ex-husband."

"If he went back up north, how can you test him?" Jaxson asked.

"I don't know. Even if Genevieve visits him and Natalie again, they might never use magic. Other than me talking to Iggy, I don't do spells on a daily basis."

"True. Let's hope neither he nor his girlfriend are guilty."

"Fingers crossed." I tried to read a book while I waited, but my mind kept wandering. A long hour later, Dom returned. I sat up straight. "Well?"

He grinned. "We have a winner."

"Really? Have a seat and tell me."

Dom carried Iggy over to the table and set him down. "Take this leash off me," Iggy complained. "Please?"

Poor thing. I removed it. "Better?"

"A piece of lettuce would make all my suffering worthwhile."

Jaxson stood. "I'll get it, your highness."

"No sign of your nemesis?" I asked.

"No. I'm betting Tippy was intimidated by big Dom here."

I don't think seagulls thought like that, but I saw no reason to argue with him. I turned to Dom. "Tell me about the interaction with Zelda."

"I waited down the street from the yarn shop for Zelda to come out. I have no idea what she was doing in there for so long, but eventually she left and headed north toward the bank."

"You followed her?"

"Actually, she came toward us. Iggy played his part very

well. We pretended as if we were out for a stroll. When we were close to Zelda, I looked up at her and smiled. Poor lady probably never gets any attention."

"Not from a young man, I bet."

"Anyway, she stopped and asked about Iggy."

"Without a hitch, our little detective looked up at her and asked Zelda what her name was. I think she was so taken aback that Iggy could talk that she answered."

"Really? That's wonderful, though I honestly had put her low on the list of potential murder suspects."

Jaxson came out with the lettuce and placed the plate in front of Iggy. "I can hear Iggy, and Dom can hear Iggy. That doesn't mean we murdered anyone. I'm also not a warlock."

"True, and she really doesn't have a good motive either, or any motive at all, really. No one would kill someone just because that person rented a storefront before they had the chance to."

Jaxson shrugged. "There could be something else involved here that we know nothing about."

"For sure. What do we do next?"

"Are there no cameras in the back of the yarn shop?" Dom asked me.

"Other than one in the front room, no. That is, there isn't one as you walk toward the back." I explained there was one facing the parking lot and two cameras in the rear of the building, but they had somehow malfunctioned.

"That sounds like a witch to me," Jaxson said. "They were high quality cameras."

"Before we jump to any conclusions, let's see if Norman Eastwick can use telekinesis to get out of jail."

"What difference does that make?" Dom asked.

"We think that Barbara was killed by someone with telekinetic abilities, not just magical skills. I can talk to Iggy, but I can't move a knitting needle with my mind."

"Gotcha."

Dom stood. "Courtney and I are going out tonight, but let me know what happens."

"Will do."

Once he left, I felt a bit empty. "Anyone up for dinner?" I asked.

"I'm going to see Gavin," Rihanna said.

I turned to Jaxson. "What about you?"

He grinned. "I'm always up for going out."

I gave him a kiss and then turned to Iggy. "What is your pleasure?"

"I'm staying here. I'm getting the sense someone is out there."

"Tippy?" I asked.

"Yes."

There were times when it wasn't worth arguing. "Okay."

Most likely, he just wanted to have a chance to visit with Aimee. I didn't think she was all too happy with Iggy spending so much time with Hugo. At some point, we'd have to get all of them together.

"Where would you like to eat?" Jaxson asked as he followed me down the outside staircase.

"How about the Magic Wand Hotel?"

His brows rose. "You usually don't suggest that place."

In part because it was expensive, and in part because old habits die hard. "It would be wise not to get into a gossip fest with anyone at this point in the investigation."

"Because?"

"Because we don't need anything to get back to any of the suspects."

He smiled. "Smart."

We headed into the hotel and went straight through the antique looking lobby to the restaurant and bar area in back. The last time we were there, we met up with the person who turned out to be the murderer in a case we were working on.

Once we were seated, we ordered a glass of wine. While I waited, I checked my phone to make sure that Steve hadn't called. Norman Eastwick should have arrived by now, unless he ran into traffic.

"Whoever killed Barbara has to be powerful," I said.

"Because he can use telekinesis?"

"Yes, but also because this person disabled the cameras from afar and then was able to open the back door without anyone seeing them."

"Are you thinking another gargoyle is involved?"

That was the only person—or rather creature—who could teleport, as far as I was aware. "Maybe."

"You're certain Genevieve is innocent?"

"Certain? No, but she is almost too naïve to be a killer."

He dipped his head. "That's your logic?"

"Yup. If none of the other suspects pan out, I'll look at her—or at Hugo to be fair."

"Great."

Since my brain was pretty much fried with all of this murder talk, we changed the subject to Dom and how it was working out with his technology learning curve going from the 1970s to the twenty-first century. Progress was hard enough to keep up with for people who'd grown up with computers, let alone if you had time traveled forward fifty years.

"He's doing great."

"Do you think he'll be ready to do some training so he can apply in the near future to the FBI again?" I asked.

"I'm not sure he wants to. Right now, he is happy being with Courtney and helping her run the store."

"Being happy is key."

"I couldn't agree more."

We discussed his brother and Andorra and then turned our attention to Hugo and Genevieve once more. "Do you think Hugo is capable of having a relationship?" I asked.

"Personally, I think it is none of our business. But if anyone can turn Hugo around, it will be Genevieve."

That was my cue to eat and enjoy the fabulous meal. Once we finished, we took a nice walk on the beach. Feeling adventurous, I slipped off my sandals so I could enjoy the slightly coarse sand on the bottom of my feet. After walking for a bit, I even dipped my toes into the Gulf.

"We need to spend more time down here," I said.

"We absolutely do." Jaxson wrapped an arm around my waist, and in silence, we walked along the coast, watching the seagulls buzz on by.

"Why do you think Iggy thinks a seagull is out to get him?" I asked.

"If I knew that, pink lady, I probably could solve this case."

I wasn't certain what that meant, but that was okay. The

warm salt air was helping to soothe all of my neurons from firing too fast.

After our walk, he escorted me back to my apartment. "Let me see if Iggy has returned," I said. "He might still be in the office. In which case, I'll rescue him."

We stepped inside where I found Iggy and Aimee deep in conversation. I stepped back into the hallway since I wanted to kiss Jaxson goodnight in peace.

"Call me if Steve contacts you," he said.

"I will."

I kissed Jaxson goodbye and stepped back inside. Before Iggy stopped his conversation with Aimee. I caught a few words, one of which was Tippy. Sheesh.

"Is Norman a warlock?" he asked, clearly deciding it was better to change the subject. I think he knew I wasn't a fan of his seagull paranoia.

"Steve hasn't called."

I left those two to finish their discussion and went into the bedroom to put on my pajamas and spend the remainder of the evening reading in bed. I'd just changed when Steve's phone call came.

"Hey. How did it go with Mr. Eastwick?"

"It didn't." Steve explained that he had arrested the poor man as per our plan. "Eastwick was so distraught he didn't even try to escape. I don't think he is our man, Glinda."

Darn. "He had such a good motive."

"I know. I can ask the ex-husband to come in, claiming that someone heard him argue with Barbara."

"You'd do that?" I couldn't believe Steve would ever falsely arrest someone—twice no less. I'm sure it had to be against the law. "That would be fantastic."

"No promises. Any other news on your end?"

"Yes." I told him that Zelda, the banker's wife, was a witch.

"Do you think she can move stuff with a wave of a hand?"

"That I don't know, but I'll work on a way to figure it out. If we can prove that Craig Simons is a warlock, I'll focus on him. He might have the most to lose."

"He might. I'll try to get a look at his financials."

"Maybe ask him point blank if he was paying alimony. If he wasn't, that lessens his chance of being guilty."

"Is that so?" I could hear the smile in his voice.

"Sorry. You know what you're doing."

"Thank you, Glinda, and good night."

"Night."

If I'd been at the office, I would have dragged out my white board and put an X through Norman Eastlake's name. At least we had one viable candidate—Zelda. Knowing who was a witch or warlock was a start, but it certainly didn't prove murder.

I texted Jaxson what Steve had said and then went back to reading my book. I had almost fallen asleep when my cell rang again. I thought it might be Jaxson, but instead it was Andorra. That meant Genevieve had news about Laura Singletary. "Hey."

"Sorry to call so late, but Genevieve just returned. She found several spell books at Laura's house."

"That's great. Did Genevieve see her do anything witchy? Like did she use telekinesis?" Not that I wasn't thrilled to have another witch candidate, but without the ability to move objects with the mind, the person probably wasn't the killer.

"No."

"Oh." I told her what Steve reported.

"It just might be Craig, the ex-husband."

"Yes, though we should check out his girlfriend, too. She could have been jealous."

"Do you want me to ask Genevieve to check her out?"

It was late. "Genevieve might not need sleep, but Natalie does. Tomorrow is soon enough."

"Okay. Let me ask you. What happens after you get your list of who has magical powers and who doesn't?"

I let out a breath. "I don't know. It's usually obvious what we need to do, but this case is different. I feel as if we're missing something."

"Don't worry. We'll figure it out."

"Yeah. We usually do. Night."

When I hung up, I was actually a little depressed. Even if we learned who had telekinetic powers, that fact alone didn't prove they were a murderer. Wanting to take my mind off of this whole affair, I picked up my book again.

When the phone rang once more, I roused from my stupor. Only this time, sunlight was blaring through the window, yet I didn't remember falling asleep.

"Are you going to answer the phone?" Iggy was tapping his foot on my bed, probably annoyed that I was shirking my duties.

I picked up my cell and checked the screen. "It's Steve." I swiped the on button. "Hello?"

"Glinda. It's Steve. Can you come to the station? Genevieve is here, and she is incredibly excited about something."

She'd already told me that Laura probably had witch abilities—or maybe she was just a wanna-be witch. "Sure. What has her so hyped up?"

"She's convinced she's found our killer."

"Who?"

"She won't say until you get here."

"Be right there."

Chapter Seventeen

DID GENEVIEVE REALLY find the killer? The only way she could have would be if she'd seen someone move an object who also had a great motive for wanting Barbara Simons dead. This monumental event had to have occurred between last night and this morning.

I quickly dressed and then called Jaxson.

"You coming into work?" Jaxson asked.

Oh, no. I hadn't even looked at the clock. When I checked, I couldn't believe I'd slept in so late. "Yes, but not now." I explained that Steve called and said Genevieve knew who the killer was.

"Who?"

"I don't know. I'm heading over to the sheriff's office now to find out."

"I'll join you. See you in a bit."

Iggy was looking up at me. "Don't even think about not taking me," he said.

I suppose he might be able to help. "Then come on."

With him in my bag, we rushed downstairs and then crossed the street to the sheriff's department. My head screamed for coffee, but I didn't have time to grab a cup. I might have to beg for some from Steve, bad though his coffee might be.

Jaxson must have sprinted across the street, because he was there when I arrived. Since Steve had invited me, I only said hello to Pearl instead of spending a bit of time to chat. I headed straight to the conference room. Andorra, Genevieve, Jaxson, Steve, and Nash were all seated. I had no idea where Rihanna was. If I had to guess, she was out taking photos since she loved the early morning light. I wouldn't be surprised if Iggy asked her to find Tippy if only to learn where Iggy's nemesis liked to hang out.

We slipped inside. This ought to be good. I slid onto the seat next to Jaxson and placed Iggy on the table. Neither Steve nor Nash even blinked at seeing my familiar.

Steve turned to Genevieve. "You have your audience. Please tell us who you think killed Barbara Simons and why."

"Okay, so I was leaving the Hex and Bones to get a breath of fresh air when I thought I spotted someone I knew enter the yarn shop."

"No one should have been there except for the new renter," Steve said.

I put the two comments together. "Are you talking about Zelda Dickens?"

"Yes," she said.

I had no idea how she knew her since Genevieve had been on top of a church for so many years. "Did you see her go to church? Is that how you knew her?" That alone wouldn't help with the woman's name.

"No."

"Genevieve," Steve said. "Can you get to the point?"

"Oh. Sure. Zelda is Barbara Lipton's aunt."

I sat there stunned for a moment, trying to figure out what that meant exactly, or rather how it impacted the case. "How does that point a finger at Zelda?"

"That I'm not sure about. Maybe some of your lady friends can ask around to see if she still has a grudge against Barbara."

This was going way too fast for me. "A grudge? About what?"

She blew out a breath. "Okay, let me start back at when I was twelve. Everything seemed normal—or at least to me it did. When I first arrived at the Lipton household, we would visit Aunt Zelda and her husband every week, and they would visit us. I have to say she's aged a lot in eighteen years."

"Most people do," I said. "I assume she didn't recognize you this time?"

"No. I grew up. Here's the thing that makes me pretty sure that Zelda killed Barbara. I'd been with the Lipton family for maybe three months when Barbara decided I wasn't the cute, fuzzy familiar that she'd expected to walk out of the forest with. So, she threw a fit." Genevieve shook her head. "That was so like her. She was a spoiled, unpleasant person, even back then. Anyway, she finally demanded that I leave."

"How did Barbara's mom react?" Steve asked.

"To my surprise, Mrs. Lipton stuck up for me. At first, that is, but then she caved after Barbara begged her to get rid of me. Barbara said that the kids at school liked me more than her, and she didn't like that."

"I imagine not. What about Mr. Lipton? What was his opinion?"

"He did whatever Barbara's mom told him." She held up

hand. "Here is the interesting part. Zelda found out about this and was horrified. She told her sister that they had to keep me. Sending me back to the orphanage was cruel and unacceptable."

"I take it they never told Zelda that you were a familiar and that you didn't come from an orphanage?" Jaxson asked.

"No. I guess it would have made Barbara look bad if Aunt Zelda found out that her niece failed at her first big spell."

I whistled. "So Zelda defended you?"

"Yes, but Barbara's mom only wanted what was best for Barbara, which was why she and her sister fought. It was ugly. Needless to say, Zelda lost, and Nancy won. After I was sent away, I never saw any of them again—until recently."

That was sad, but I wasn't seeing a motive for murder.

Steve pushed back his chair. "Let me ask my grandmother to come in here. She might have heard about that scuttlebutt back then. I always like to have a different perspective." He left to speak with Pearl.

After Steve spoke with his grandmother for a moment, she nodded and then followed him back into the conference room. He motioned that she take a seat.

"Ooh, this is so thrilling. My grandson never lets me come in here."

"Don't get too excited, Gram. Do you know anything about the tiff between Zelda Dickens and her sister, Nancy Lipton, many years ago?"

"An argument? I recall something, but not the details. I've heard they didn't speak at all—even after Nancy became ill. She died, you know. It's why Zelda is a little bitter." Pearl scrunched up her nose. "Or rather a lot bitter."

"No, I didn't know Barbara's mom had passed. I wasn't living here at the time." Steve sat up straighter in his chair. "Gram, do you think you could ask around? The details of that family spat is really important to our case."

She narrowed her eyes. "What is going on here?"

"I promise to tell you everything, just not now. Please?"

Pearl lifted her chin. "Fine. I'll make some calls."

While she sounded a bit miffed that her grandson didn't fill in all of the gaps, the sparkle in her eyes told a different story. I wanted to ask her for some coffee, but she had important business to attend to. I could wait.

Once Pearl left, Steve turned to Genevieve.

"What happened after you spotted Zelda?" Steve asked.

"Being curious, I wanted to learn a little more about what she'd been up to, so I kind of, sort of, cloaked myself and watched her in the store." She sounded guilty, almost as if she finally understood that spying on a person was wrong.

"I'm assuming that Zelda didn't sense your presence?" Steve asked.

"No! I stayed for quite a while, too. That's when I saw it."

Genevieve had a knack for dragging out a story. "Saw what?" I asked.

She held up her hands. "Zelda had a cane when she went into the store, but she never used it while inside. I think the cane might have been her way to get people's sympathy."

"Maybe she needed it when she had to walk a long distance," I suggested.

"Maybe, but all I know is that she'd been working in the back for a while. When she needed to go to the front, she held out her hand like this, and the cane flew into her palm. She might not have wanted anyone on the sidewalk to see her inside without it."

"Holy moly. Zelda was able to harness telekinesis?" That shocked me to the core.

"Yes." Genevieve leaned back in her seat and surveyed the room. "What do you want me to do next?"

"Get her to confess to killing Barbara." I laughed, because I was only kidding. I still wasn't convinced there was a motive for murder.

"How?" Genevieve sounded serious.

Steve cleared his throat. "If we really think that Zelda is guilty of this crime, we need to understand her motive. My grandmother will put the word out to her friends for information about this big argument, unless any of you think the ex-husband knows the story."

No one said anything. Finally, I had to say something. "Just because Zelda had a beef with her sister years ago over her young niece's bad behavior, it doesn't mean she'd harm Barbara now. So what if Zelda has the magical talent to do so?"

Jaxson placed a hand on my arm. "Let Steve handle this. He'll ask for our help if he needs it."

Darn. I was being too bossy, but I doubted Steve could do much without our help. I looked over at him. "It's your show."

"Thank you, Jaxson and Glinda. How about we find out from my grandmother the latest gossip first. I don't think time is of the essence, since Zelda won't have any idea we're on to her—assuming she's our murderer. I'll contact all of you when I learn something."

That worked for me. "Great."

Even though we'd been dismissed, that didn't mean I was going to let this go. I picked up Iggy, who'd been surprisingly quiet, and we followed everyone out. As I left, I was happy to see Pearl was on the phone, doing her part to solve this crime.

Once outside, I turned to Jaxson. "I'm going to chat with Andorra and Genevieve. Want to join me?"

"Absolutely. Someone has to keep you ladies in line."

I stood on my toes and kissed his cheek. "You are the best."

As soon as we went inside the store, Iggy crawled out of my purse. I didn't need to ask him where he was going. I knew. He made a beeline to the back where Hugo was.

Since Elizabeth and Bertha were tending the store, Andorra motioned we follow her to the back. She seemed to understand we needed to plot.

After arranging the folding chairs into a circle, all of us but Iggy and Hugo sat down. I turned to Genevieve since I had the sense she knew more than she'd stated to the sheriff. "Why again do you think Zelda killed Barbara? I agree that she might have had the ability, but why do it?"

"I can't say exactly, but there was a lot of fighting between the sisters and with Barbara. I didn't like Barbara at all once she told me that she wanted me out of her life, or should I say, demanded that I stay out of it. But I didn't kill her." No one said anything. "You have to believe me. If I'd wanted to harm Barbara, I would have asked Hugo to do it."

Andorra sucked in a breath. "Genevieve, that's terrible. Please don't ever ask him to do anything like that."

Genevieve looked over at Hugo and listened for a bit.

"Fine. I'll tell Andorra first."

I was glad one of them had some common sense. I couldn't comprehend what that kind of rejection would do to a person—especially to a young girl, though maybe it didn't affect Genevieve as much since she wasn't totally human. Thank goodness she really hadn't been required to go into an orphanage. She would have terrorized those poor children.

"The argument between Zelda and her sister happened a long time ago," I said. "Why do you think Zelda would take revenge against Barbara now?"

"I don't know."

The pieces weren't lining up. "Is it possible that Zelda killed Barbara by mistake? The flying knitting needle could have been a result of an errant hand motion."

"What do you mean?" Jaxson asked.

"People do stupid stuff in the heat of the moment. Tempers flare. Consider you're Zelda. You're at the later stages of your life, and your health might not be the best. All you want is to have a shop where you can socialize with other women."

Andorra nodded. "Right, and then along comes someone who steals the store right out from under you. It wouldn't matter if Barbara had any idea that Zelda wanted it or not."

"I agree. The two could have been chatting, and Zelda might have gestured wildly. Suddenly, the knitting needle flew into the air and...well, you know the rest."

"No," Iggy said a moment later.

"No?"

"Hugo said it doesn't work that way. It takes concentration to move an object."

"Oh." I looked over at Hugo. "Thanks for clarifying

that."

Genevieve crossed her arms. "Since Nancy Lipton is dead, we can't ask her. The only solution is to confront Zelda."

"What? No. Do you plan on asking her point blank if she killed Barbara? I hate to break it to you, but she isn't going to confess even if she is guilty."

Genevieve smiled. "I could make her?" She then looked over at Hugo. "Or I could ask my trusty sidekick to get her to confess."

"Coerced confessions won't hold up in court," Jaxson informed her.

It only worked before for us because of a complicated spell.

She slumped in her seat. Just then Steve walked into the back room.

"I thought I'd find you all here," Steve announced.

We'd just left him. "Did you find out something?"

"In a way. According to one of Dolly's friends, Zelda and her sister had a falling out over an adoption gone wrong." He glanced over at Genevieve who smiled sweetly. "Anyway, Zelda has always blamed Barbara for putting that wedge in the family. Since Zelda never had any children, she thought she and Barbara could bond, but that was destroyed when the family sent Genevieve back to the orphanage—or told Zelda they sent her there."

"Did Pearl find out if Zelda knew for sure that Fifi LaRue was her niece? People change a lot from the age of twelve," I asked.

Genevieve answered instead of Steve. "I don't know about that, but I'm pretty sure Zelda didn't recognize me. At least, she didn't act as if she did."

"I wonder if that was why Barbara changed her name. She didn't want Zelda recognizing her," I said.

"That could be," he said.

Genevieve eyes lit up. "What if I can get Zelda to show us her telekinetic skills, and we record it on camera?"

Chapter Eighteen

STEVE SHOOK HIS head. "Recording someone doing something illegal won't hold up in court if the other person is unaware you're doing it." He explained how the law was a bit unclear in some circumstances and that there were exceptions. "For example, if this case involved crossing state lines, we could turn the video over to the FBI, and all might be good. Unfortunately, that's not the case."

"There are cameras inside the store," Jaxson reminded us. "If Genevieve can get her to confess in the main showroom, would that be admissible?"

"I believe Heath Richards pointed out those cameras to her, so yes, that would work."

Genevieve smiled. "Okay. I'll lead her into the main room and then distract her."

"How?" Steve asked.

"I can disappear right in front of her or else I'll move an object." Genevieve looked so hopeful.

"Please don't," Steve said. "You'd be hounded for the rest of your life if people found out about your talents."

She looked over at Hugo, but he shrugged. "Maybe, but I want to try." Genevieve turned back to Steve. "I know. I'll tell her I'm that little twelve-year-old girl who was abandoned. I can thank her for sticking up for me and doing away with Barbara. I'll even tell her that I was the one who strung the pink yarn all over the store in the hopes it would drive Barbara out of town."

Steve looked around. "I suppose we have nothing to lose with that. I doubt anything will come of it though."

Genevieve clapped, acting more like the twelve-year-old girl than the woman she'd become. "When can we do this?"

"Not until Zelda returns to store. Maybe you can zoom in and out throughout the day. When you see her, stop in at the office and I'll outfit you with a camera. Note, the camera is merely to allow me to make sure things don't get out of hand."

She grinned. "I won't let you all down."

With a good plan ready to execute, we all left. Jaxson, Iggy, and I headed back to the office, while Andorra and Genevieve returned to the show room. "Are you up for some food?" I asked Jaxson. "I need breakfast."

He kissed the top of my head. "Always. Do you have a place in mind?"

It's not like we had a ton of options. "I think it will be safest at the Tiki Hut. Aunt Fern has probably received a call from Pearl, but she'll understand if we can't discuss the case."

"Then let's go. We can brainstorm ways this plan might fail so we can offer suggestions."

AROUND TWO, STEVE called and told us we needed to head over to his office. It was time. When we arrived, Pearl told us to go into the conference room where Steve was set up.

He turned the dark monitor toward us. "We can hear and see almost everything. Or we will, once she turns on her camera."

"Can you communicate with Genevieve?" I asked. "There might be something we need her to ask Zelda."

"Not directly. An earbud might be noticed, but Andorra will be arriving shortly with Hugo. She believes he can relay any information to her."

"Hugo is coming here?" Iggy asked.

"That's what Steve just said," I told him. "Now, shh."

A few seconds later, Andorra and Hugo entered the station. He stopped and looked around at the new surroundings until Andorra motioned him forward. I'd have to ask her when the last time Hugo had been outside of the Hex and Bones.

Once they entered the conference room, Iggy crawled across the table to the two empty chairs and waited for his friend.

"Do we know when Genevieve plans on speaking with Zelda?" Steve asked her, his voice thick with tension.

"She's on her way there now," Andorra said.

As if Genevieve had heard Andorra, the camera attached to the button on her shirt clicked on. "Is this thing on?" She jiggled it.

Genevieve was in the back alley where the video cameras to the yarn shop still weren't working. She looked up. "Great. Thanks, Hugo."

She heard him! I wasn't sure he could communicate with her when they were so far apart even though they were fairly close emotionally. I know he'd been able to use mental telepathy with Andorra when she'd gone missing, but Genevieve wasn't his host.

One second, Genevieve was outside the yarn shop, and the next, she was on the other side of the back door. I hoped that Zelda didn't see her appear out of thin air. After looking around, Genevieve stepped into the room where we'd held the séance. Who should be there but Zelda.

The older woman planted a hand on her chest. "How did you get in here?"

We figured Zelda would ask that so we'd prepared Genevieve with how to answer. "I came through the back. I'm working over at the Hex and Bones and was out back when I saw your security door was ajar. You should get that fixed."

"Oh. Ah, thank you." Zelda walked forward without her cane—a cane that was against the wall behind her. "I'm Zelda Dickens. I just rented this place after the last owner, um, died."

Just like we planned, Genevieve held out her arms in a welcoming motion. "You don't recognize me?"

Zelda studied Genevieve. "Should I? Do you bank with us?"

"No. I'm Genevieve, Barbara Lipton's friend from long ago."

Her eyes nearly teared up. "Genevieve? You're okay?" No one expected Zelda to embrace her.

"Yes, I'm fine." She almost giggled. Either Genevieve was an excellent actress or she was genuinely pleased by Zelda's welcome.

"Tell me how you've been," Zelda said. "You look good."

Genevieve sneezed about ten times in a row. "I'm sorry. It's really dusty back here. Can we sit out in front and chat?"

"Sure. Grab those two chairs."

I had to hand it to Genevieve for creating that diversion. It wasn't what I'd expected. Once they sat down, Genevieve told a sad tale of living with several different families. I honestly didn't think she was capable of storytelling like that, but she sounded convincing to me, and I knew none of it was true.

"Did you get to talk with Barbara before she passed?" Zelda asked.

"Yes and no. I have been angry my entire life because of that sad, nasty woman." Genevieve tapped her chest. "I was the one who strung pink yarn all over her shop. I heard Barbara was furious." She tittered.

Zelda leaned forward. "I heard that, too, and I'm glad."

"You and your sister never made up?"

"No. I think Nancy wanted to, but Barbara convinced her mom that I was poison. Me! I'm the one who wanted you to stay. I was not the bad guy here."

"I know. I am forever grateful to you for standing up for me. All I can say is that Barbara had it coming. I'm glad she was murdered."

Zelda pressed her lips together. "Promise you won't say anything if I tell you something?"

Genevieve crossed her heart. She must have learned that from when she and Barbara were kids. "My lips are sealed."

"What happened to Barbara was an accident, but I'm not sorry."

I grabbed Jaxson's arm. "Did Zelda just confess to killing

Barbara?"

"I don't know. Shh."

I focused on what the two women were saying.

"What happened?" Genevieve said.

"I wanted to see if maybe we could let bygones be bygones. After all, it had been eighteen years since Barbara sent you away. I was mad at how she'd treated you, but I was hoping Barbara had changed."

"She did. She changed her name to Fifi! I know she loved France, but that was over the top, right?"

"I couldn't agree more. Anyway, I wanted to put that behind us. I'm not getting any younger, and I never had children. I thought Barbara and I could patch things up, especially now that her mom is gone."

"Barbara was too mean to agree to anything like that," Genevieve mumbled.

"So I found out," Zelda said. "I waited until she'd closed up one evening, and then I came in through the back. As soon as she saw me, she knew who I was. I can still see it. She picked up a knitting needle and waved it at me, shouting at me to leave."

"That's terrible. She didn't listen to what you had to say?"

"No. You know how stubborn she could be. Then she just lost it."

"Did Barbara actually threaten you with the knitting needle?"

Zelda clamped a hand on her own neck as if she was reliving a moment. "Yes. She lifted the needle and came at me. I had to defend myself."

"I can't imagine how horrible that was. What did you

do?"

"I did this." One second Zelda was sitting there as calm as could be, and the next, she swept a hand and made another knitting needle fly through the air.

I sucked in a breath. Had there been a camera pointed at Barbara the night she died, it would have been déjà vu all over again. Only this time, instead of the needle penetrating Genevieve, she disappeared before it could. The needle harmlessly pinged off a shelf and fell to the ground.

I wasn't sure what had occurred, but apparently neither did Zelda. She looked around. "Genevieve?"

Our resident gargoyle appeared next to her. "Trying to kill me too?"

"No, it happened again. Can't you see I have no control over my powers?"

I studied those in this room to see if anyone bought her story, but I couldn't tell. All eyes were focused on the screen.

I expected Genevieve to accept what Zelda was claiming had happened, only she didn't seem to be believing a word of it. "If you have no control over your powers, how did you manage to disable the cameras in back?" Genevieve held up her hand. "And just so you know, we are recording this conversation. If you have any chance of avoiding a long time in jail, I suggest you tell the truth."

There was no way that idea came from Genevieve. When Hugo leaned back in his seat and smiled, I could see he was feeding her those lines. Go Hugo!

"That is ridiculous. I did no such thing." Zelda ran her gaze up and down Genevieve's body. "Who are you?"

"*Moi?* I am not some orphan who your sister adopted. I

can't believe she didn't tell you that I was Barbara's familiar. While her spell was for a cat, I showed up instead."

"That's...that's ridiculous."

Genevieve grinned, clearly enjoying this interaction. "Is it now? To further blow your mind, I am a gargoyle."

Zelda huffed until Genevieve actually transformed into a stone statue. At the sight of that change, Zelda passed out. A few seconds later, both Nash and Hunter Ashwell, Penny's boyfriend, rushed into the store from both entrances.

Nash tapped the microphone on his shirt. "Steve, maybe you should call for help."

"Will do," he said.

Steve called for an ambulance, while Nash and Hunter remained by her side, I'm sure ready to put her in cuffs should she awake. As for Genevieve, she remained in her statue form in the middle of the room. She was probably waiting for them to leave before she turned human again.

"Hugo," I said, "you can tell Genevieve that Nash and Hunter will keep her secret. Both have just as big of a one themselves."

A few seconds later, she was fully human once more. She looked up at the camera in the shop. "How did I do?"

Steve smiled. "Hugo, tell her she was amazing."

When he relayed the information, she clapped. A second later, she was in the room with us. "Did we get everything we needed?"

The joy in her voice made me smile.

"It's possible," Steve said. "Your camera was merely to help us understand what was going on. It's the camera in the main room that will incriminate Zelda, unless the jury believes it was self-defense. It will be her word against a dead woman's. I'll ask Heath Richards to confirm that he told her about the camera in the showroom. It means she had to know she was being recorded the whole time. Let me call him and ask if we can get the footage."

Steve made the call and told Heath what had happened. "I'm afraid so... I know it's bad luck losing two tenants in a row, but I'm sure you'll find someone soon." He made sure Heath had told Zelda about the cameras both in the front of the store as well as the one in the main area. She clearly knew there were cameras in back. "If would be great if you could send the feed to me as soon as you can."

I imagine Heath would need to call the security company. Even though Zelda knew about the camera in the main room. most likely, she was too distracted to remember it was there.

He disconnected. "Looks like Zelda will be pleading her case in our human court. It could be self-defense in the death of Barbara, but it looked like she was trying to kill Genevieve. The fact that the needle landed harmlessly on the ground might keep her out of jail. The part where Genevieve disappeared needs to be deleted."

I was just happy knowing that Barbara Lipton's killer had been caught. "We should try her in the court of her peers," I suggested. "Then we can get her for one murder and one attempted murder. We could have Hugo or rather Genevieve testify that one needs to concentrate to move an object."

"Given who her husband is, I doubt we could do that, but I'll try."

Chapter Nineteen

One week later

JAXSON AND I were sitting in the office enjoying a tea, Rihanna was out with Gavin doing whatever, and Iggy was with Aimee. Now that Hugo said he would remain human—or rather could change into his human form whenever Iggy was around—my familiar was one happy camper.

"Do you think Zelda will win her self-defense plea?" I asked. The preliminary hearing was scheduled for next week.

"That's hard to say. I don't think they can use any of the footage of her attempting to shoot a needle at Genevieve."

"I figured, but how can she explain her ability to stab Barbara with such force?" I slumped against the sofa. "I wish Steve could have her tried in the other court system. The witches and warlocks don't care about our legal technicalities. The fact that Genevieve was able to disappear at the right moment and avoid being stabbed wouldn't matter. Zelda meant to kill her."

"I know, but it's not to be. I heard Sam Dickens hired some top lawyer from Tampa to defend his wife."

"I hope they throw the book at her," I said.

"Me, too, but I don't think that will happen." He leaned

back. "I know it doesn't matter now, but what did your mother say about why your pink pendant turned blue."

"She wasn't sure. We discussed it and decided it must have related to electricity or some ability to generate heat."

He nodded. "Makes sense."

I sipped on my tea. "I've been thinking."

Jaxson smiled. "Already? The case is barely cold."

"Funny. You know we have quite a pile of money that we haven't figured out what to do with."

"It's a lot, but we will run out someday, especially if you're planning on buying a mansion or something."

"No, silly. I love my life the way it is, but Heath Richards wants out of being a landlord."

Jaxson nodded. "I heard he put that whole strip up for sale."

I twisted toward Jaxson. "Right. The next buyer might increase all of the rents. I'm not sure that Silas can afford more than what he is paying. While Bertha can, why should she?"

Jaxson's brows pinched. "What are you getting at?"

I probably should have figured out a better way to approach this topic, but I couldn't think of one, so I decided just to say it. "What if we buy the strip mall?"

"Buy as in be landlords?"

"Yes, that would give us a steady income. All of the major repairs have already been completed. I wouldn't have to worry about charging clients when we help them. What do you think?"

Jaxson slid closer to me on the sofa. "If this is what you want to do, I'll support you."

"Really?"

He grinned. "Did you think I would say no?"

"Maybe. It's possible it isn't the best financial decision."

He ran a knuckle down my cheek. "Since when have I ever really cared about us making the soundest decisions? As long as you're happy, I'm happy."

My heart totally melted. "Did I ever tell you that I loved you?"

"No! Are you sure?"

"Absolutely."

Just as Jaxson leaned over to kiss me, guess who ran in through the cat door? Yup. Iggy.

"I'm done. I'm never going outside again, because if I do, look out Tippy."

When I spotted my familiar, I really tried not to laugh, but I failed miserably. Iggy's head was covered in bird poop. "I'm sorry, but how do you know it was Tippy?"

"I saw him, but if it wasn't him, he orchestrated the attack."

I disengaged from our embrace and stood. "I think someone needs a bath."

"That only adds insult to injury. I'm putting Tippy on notice. He is going to pay."

I didn't even get the chance to pick him up before Iggy marched straight to the bathroom, and I followed.

"I'll be waiting here when you get out," Jaxson said with too much joy in his voice.

Despite the indignation Iggy had just gone through, life was looking up for us all!

I hope you enjoyed Knotted Up In Pink Yarn. I had such fun creating Genevieve. I always felt that poor Hugo needed someone to help him through life besides Iggy. Don't worry, this duo will be staying around for a while.

What's next? It's Glinda's twenty-eighth birthday, and she gets a surprise present. GHOSTS AND PINK CANDLES explores what happens when people of magic die.

Buy on Amazon or read for FREE on Kindle Unlimited

Don't forget to sign up for my Cozy Mystery newsletter *to learn about my discounts and upcoming releases. If you prefer to only receive notices regarding my releases, follow me on BookBub.*
http://smarturl.it/VellaDayNL
bookbub.com/authors/vella-day

Here is a sneak peak of book 14: Ghosts and Pink Candles

"HAPPY BIRTHDAY TO you. Happy birthday to you. Happy birthday, dear Glinda, happy birthday to you. How o-old are you?"

My ears rang from the off-key voices—two of which belonged to my parents. Both were tone deaf, which made birthdays a little painful. However, now that that song was over, I could focus on the good stuff.

In front of me was a huge two-layer chocolate cake with chocolate and pink frosting. My aunt had made it—pastries were her specialty—and she'd rimmed the bottom layer with cherries, because she knew I loved them. The sprinkles were a nice added touch, too.

Almost everyone my aunt and mother had invited to this party had shown up, and I hoped there would be enough dessert for the twenty-plus people at The Tiki Hut Grill. Knowing my efficient Aunt Fern, she had another cake in the back just in case.

"Blow out the candles, sweetie," my mother urged.

Even though I was now twenty-eight, there were only five candles on top, which was fine by me. Because there was something rather unsanitary about having breath pour over a cake, I wet my fingers and doused the flames quickly. I might be a witch, but I didn't have the power to extinguish the flames with a wave of a hand or by tossing out a quick spell. That talent belonged to someone else.

The rather sweet sulfur scent that I pleasantly associated with séances and Christmas teased my nostrils. I might be the only one, but I liked the smell.

"Did you make a wish?" my mother asked.

No. In truth, I didn't believe that birthday wishes came true, so why make them? My mom, however, was a true believer. She also was a true believer in the Wizard of Oz, so you be the judge about her. "Sure, but I'm not telling you what I wished for."

She grinned. "Whatever it is, I hope it comes true."

"Me, too." It might if I'd made one.

"Are you going to cut the cake, open the presents, or just stare at everything?" My boyfriend, Jaxson Harrison, fully understood that I was prone to daydreaming.

He was the love of my life, despite our relationship not starting out under the best of circumstances. After a rather tumultuous beginning, we learned to appreciate each other's talents. Turns out, Jaxson was the ying to my yang. Who knew? As a result of how well we complemented each other, we started The Pink Iguana Sleuth agency a year ago. I like to think we've helped a lot of people in that time.

"I'm just admiring Aunt Fern's handiwork." I turned to my aunt. "Why don't you cut the cake? You know I'd just make a mess."

She and my mom didn't have to nod with such force—and my mother's eye roll was totally unnecessary—but I wasn't offended in the least. I could take orders and serve food, but preparing a meal or baking a cake wasn't my forte.

"Sure dear," my aunt said.

"And Mom, can you pass the plates around?"

"Of course."

In quick order, my aunt cut the cake into perfectly even pieces, something I never could have achieved. As my mom passed out the dessert to the guests, I checked the assortment of friends who were there. They ranged from the sheriff and his deputy, along with both of their girlfriends, to the many gossip queens in town—which included my Aunt Fern. Naturally, my cousin, Rihanna was there with her boyfriend, Gavin, who was the medical examiner's son. Considering Witch's Cove was a small town, it didn't surprise me that everyone seemed to be connected to someone else either by blood or by job.

My aunt had cordoned off the back patio of her restaurant, including the Tiki Hut bar itself, for our party. This venue was spectacular in large part because the restaurant sat on an expansive white beach on the Gulf of Mexico. The festivities were being held after sunset, which meant the lights from the nearby boats, set against the backdrop of the Florida summer sky, twinkled in the distance. The warm, slightly salty scented breeze wafted off the water, creating a relaxing and calm environment.

Since no one was mopping sweat off their foreheads, the guests seemed to be comfortable on the outdoor patio. And yes, I had asked Aunt Fern to put several bottles of bug spray on the table, just in case.

Should the partygoers choose to imbibe, drinks were free tonight.

Once we had our cake in hand, we all took a seat at the long table that could easily handle twenty-five people. Only after everyone finished eating did I plan to open the presents. It didn't seem to matter that I asked people not to buy me anything. They all did. From the shape and size of the gifts, a few appeared to be bottles of wine, which I was happy to have.

I sat next to Jaxson, of course. My talking pink iguana familiar, Iggy, decided not to come. He understood a few of my friends might be a bit squeamish when it came to seeing an animal on the table. Iggy didn't see himself as anything other than human, but my nine-pound wonder was not one of us, despite his ability to communicate.

My mom and dad who ran the funeral home next door sat across from me. Since they always seemed to be busy, it was really nice to be with them for an evening.

Next to my mom was Penny Carsted, the woman I had waitressed with for over three years. She was with her beau,

Hunter Ashwell, who happened to be the forest ranger, as well as one of our resident werewolves—though few in town knew that about him.

"How's the landlord business going?" my mom asked, jarring me out of my reverie.

"No problems so far, though remember, we just signed the papers a few weeks ago."

When the owner of the building across the street decided he wanted nothing more to do with the issues of this town, he put the strip of stores up for sale. Since Jaxson and I had been paid extremely well for our most bizarre case—long story—we decided (okay, I had suggested) that we buy the entire strip of stores on the main street. I feared an unknown landlord might come in and impose high rents on these hard working people. Not only that, being the owner would guarantee us a monthly income.

"Have you rented the yarn shop space yet?" my mom asked.

The first owner left due to family issues, and the next owner was murdered. I hope the new owner would have better luck. "Not yet."

"I'm hoping a computer store will want to rent the space." Jaxson held up a hand. "And in case either of you hear of someone with technological abilities interested in a storefront, please send him our way."

My mom smiled. She understood Jaxson's penchant for all things that had to do with computers. "Will do."

Jaxson was amazing with technology-based items. He could find almost any snippet of information on a person that we needed—within legal limits, of course. Without his help, our business might not have succeeded.

"Glinda, what would you like to see occupy that space?" my mom asked.

That was easy. "You know I love books, but I understand that bookstores aren't very profitable. Honestly, I just want a good owner." Way to skirt the issue, right? And by a good owner, I meant one who paid attention to things—which many people would call a gossip. Hey, what can I say? It's the gas to our sleuthing engine.

"Good luck dear."

We chatted about the funeral business—never a real cheery or appropriate topic for a party—so when I noticed people had finished their dessert, I nodded to Jaxson. It was his cue to tell me to open the presents.

He stood and tapped a fork against his glass to get everyone's attention. "Okay everyone, time for the good stuff—for Glinda, that is. Then to the *real* good stuff." He nodded to the open bar, and everyone chuckled.

I walked to the end of the table where an embarrassingly large number of gifts were piled high. "You guys shouldn't have."

Naturally, that was everyone's cue to tell me how much I deserved it. What can I say? I had nice friends. I honestly wasn't sure what to open first, so I picked up a card. "It's from Maude."

Maude Daniels ran the tea shop next door. I opened it and sucked in a breath. "It's a gift card for ten teas. Thank you. That's very generous of you."

"Nonsense. This way, you'll be sure to stop in often," she said with a smile.

How sweet, but I knew it was her code for wanting to gossip, which was fine by me. I spent the next ten minutes opening almost all of my gifts, one of which was another gift card from my favorite coffee shop, run by Maude's twin sister, Miriam. Those two were highly competitive.

Next, I picked up a pretty package wrapped in the candy store's, Broomsticks and Gumdrops, signature paper. I ripped it off. I should have saved it but I was too excited to see what was inside. "It's from Courtney and Dominic. Thank you."

"You're welcome!"

Courtney Higgins was the candy store owner from across the street, and Dominic Geno was her boyfriend. I lifted the lid and nearly gasped. Layers of chocolate ringed a pile of pink gumdrops. "This is amazing."

"Enjoy."

"Oh, I'll it enjoy it all right. The hard part will be not eating it at one sitting."

The crowd laughed. The next was a gift from my cousin, Rihanna. She gave me a pink and black short-sleeved shirt, which was awesome, because pink was my signature color, and the black represented her favorite color. "I love it."

I purposefully left the two gifts from the most important people to last. I picked up the one from my parents.

"Before you open it," Mom said, "you need to know that this is from Nana."

"Nana?" My grandmother had passed away a few years ago. True, she would often show up in her ghost form at various times, but I didn't think she was able to buy something wherever witches went when they died.

"Yes. I was rooting through my closet looking for a book,

when I came across this box. When I opened it, I remembered her telling me that this was for you. I'm sorry I took so long to give it to you."

"That's okay. I have it now." Anything from my grandmother was wonderful. The only thing I had of hers was my magical pink pendant.

I tore off the pink paper to reveal a small jewelry box. When I opened it, my breath caught at the beauty of the ring. I swear the pink diamond on my necklace heated in response. I always told myself that it was my grandmother's way of letting me know she was close by.

The pink diamond in this ring was surrounded by an ornate gold setting. "It's beautiful. Do you know if it has any *special* properties?"

I was referring to magic of course. My necklace had plenty, but I didn't know about this ring.

"I never asked Mom. She just said it was for you."

Excited, I slipped it on. Before I had the chance to admire it further, something really, really strange happened. It had to be the bank of clouds floating off of the Gulf moving toward me, because there was no way I was seeing by a boatload of ghosts. The issue was that while they might have been see-through like clouds, these had faces. Did clouds have eyes, a nose, and a mouth? I swear several of them were even smiling.

"Glinda?" Jaxson placed a hand on my wrist. "Are you okay?"

No, I wasn't okay. If I had had anything to drink besides iced tea, I would have thought I was in an alcohol induced stupor. I didn't want to explain what happened for fear I'd end up making a scene. "Yeah, I'm good."

I immediately removed the ring and placed it back in its case. Like a flash, the ghosts—I mean the clouds—disappeared. That unnerved me, but I smiled anyway, trying to act as if all was well.

"You have one more to open." My boyfriend handed me a small present that looked similar to the ring box I'd just opened.

My pulse soared. *Calm down, Glinda.* If this contained an engagement ring, Jaxson would be on one knee, right? I carefully removed the pretty paper and then opened the blue velvet box. I gasped when I saw the diamond earrings. Contrary to what I'd just hoped for, I was not disappointed in the least—okay maybe just a little bit—but these earrings were spectacular. I looked up at Jaxson. "This is too much."

"Why? You deserve it, and it goes with your diamond bracelet." He nodded to what was on my wrist.

Of course, that bracelet was fake, and I imagine these earrings were not. I set the box down. "I want to try them on."

My ears were already pierced, so slipping them through the holes was easy. Once in, I looked around, posing with the bracelet.

"They are perfect," Jaxson said. "Just like you."

When I stood on my toes and kissed him, the group applauded. "You are the best," I whispered in his ear.

Jaxson leaned back and grinned. "All right everyone. Now, the real party begins."

I wanted to tell him about seeing the ghosts, but maybe that whole event had been my imagination. The ring had been a gift from my Nana, and imagining I was seeing her friends allowed me to be closer to her—if only for a few seconds.

For the next few hours, I chatted with everyone. The only two notable friends who had not come were our two gargoyle shifters. Witch's Cove sure was collecting—if that was the right word—a rather strange assortment of people, but I adored them all.

Because I was still a bit shaken from my sighting, I stuck to iced tea. If I downed a glass or two of wine, I didn't trust myself not to blab to everyone what I'd seen.

When people started to leave, I hugged each of them goodbye and thanked them for their wonderful present. When the place cleared out, I gathered my gifts as the busboys descended, whisking away the plates and glasses.

"I'll help take these up to your place," Jaxson said.

"Thanks."

Between the two of us, we managed to carry them through the restaurant and up the back staircase to my apartment. To say the least, its location was convenient. Jaxson slipped the keys from my nearly full hands and opened the door.

Iggy was there, sitting on his stool, looking out of the window. He turned to me. "How was the party?"

I couldn't tell if he was upset or not that he'd missed it, but he'd been the one to decide it was best if he stayed home. "Great, but strange."

Jaxson placed the gifts on the coffee table. "I knew something was off with you. Let me get us some coffee, and you can tell me what happened down there."

I held up a hand. "No coffee for me. I'm about to float away as it is."

"Mind if I fix a cup for myself?"

"Go ahead."

Iggy hopped off his stool and waddled after Jaxson. "Can you get me some lettuce?"

Iggy took after me—he was always hungry. I dropped onto the sofa still trying to figure out if I was crazy or not. A few minutes later, Jaxson came out carrying a steaming mug, placed it on the nearly full table, and then sat next to me.

"Tell me what happened."

He could read me well. "Please don't think I'm losing it, but when I put on the ring from my grandmother, I saw a slew of ghosts floating around me." There. I'd said it.

"Ghosts?"

"Yes, ghosts. Sure, I've seen my share in the past, but usually it is during a séance, or if they need me to solve their murder." That had happened once or twice in the past.

"Can I see this ring?" Jaxson was probably just trying to calm me down, but I appreciated it anyway. I located the box and handed it to him.

"Don't get your hopes up. You won't see any ghosts since you're not a warlock."

"I know." He opened it, and when he lifted the ring out of the case, he froze. Jaxson looked around. "No freakin' way."

Pick up Ghosts and Pink Candles on AMAZON

THE END

A WITCH'S COVE MYSTERY (Paranormal Cozy Mystery)
PINK Is The New Black (book 1)
A PINK Potion Gone Wrong (book 2)
The Mystery of the PINK Aura (book 3)
Box Set (books 1-3)
Sleuthing In The PINK (book 4)
Not in The PINK (book 5)
Gone in the PINK of an Eye (book 6)
Box Set (books 4-6)
The PINK Pumpkin Party (book 7)
Mistletoe with a PINK Bow (book 8)
The Magical PINK Pendant (book 9)
The Poisoned PINK Punch (book 10)
PINK Smoke and Mirrors (book 11)
Broomsticks and PINK Gumdrops (book 12)
Knotted Up In PINK Yarn (book 13)
Ghosts and PINK Candles (book 14)
Pilfered Pink Pearls (book 15)
The Case of the Stolen Pink Tombstone (book 16)

SILVER LAKE SERIES (3 OF THEM)
(1). HIDDEN REALMS OF SILVER LAKE (Paranormal Romance)
Awakened By Flames (book 1)
Seduced By Flames (book 2)
Kissed By Flames (book 3)
Destiny In Flames (book 4)
Box Set (books 1-4)
Passionate Flames (book 5)
Ignited By Flames (book 6)

Touched By Flames (book 7)
Box Set (books 5-7)
Bound By Flames (book 8)
Fueled By Flames (book 9)
Scorched By Flames (book 10)

(2). **FOUR SISTERS OF FATE: HIDDEN REALMS OF SILVER LAKE** (Paranormal Romance)
Poppy (book 1)
Primrose (book 2)
Acacia (book 3)
Magnolia (book 4)
Box Set (books 1-4)
Jace (book 5)
Tanner (book 6)

(3). **WERES AND WITCHES OF SILVER LAKE**
(Paranormal Romance)
A Magical Shift (book 1)
Catching Her Bear (book 2)
Surge of Magic (book 3)
The Bear's Forbidden Wolf (book 4)
Her Reluctant Bear (book 5)
Freeing His Tiger (book 6)
Protecting His Wolf (book 7)
Waking His Bear (book 8)
Melting Her Wolf's Heart (book 9)
Her Wolf's Guarded Heart (book 10)
His Rogue Bear (book 11)
Box Set (books 1-4)
Box Set (books 5-8)

Reawakening Their Bears (book 12)

OTHER PARANORMAL SERIES
PACK WARS (Paranormal Romance)
Training Their Mate (book 1)
Claiming Their Mate (book 2)
Rescuing Their Virgin Mate (book 3)
Box Set (books 1-3)
Loving Their Vixen Mate (book 4)
Fighting For Their Mate (book 5)
Enticing Their Mate (book 6)
Box Set (books 1-4)
Complete Box Set (books 1-6)

HIDDEN HILLS SHIFTERS (Paranormal Romance)
An Unexpected Diversion (book 1)
Bare Instincts (book 2)
Shifting Destinies (book 3)
Embracing Fate (book 4)
Promises Unbroken (book 5)
Bare 'N Dirty (book 6)
Hidden Hills Shifters Complete Box Set (books 1-6)

CONTEMPORARY SERIES
MONTANA PROMISES (Full length contemporary Romance)
Promises of Mercy (book 1)
Foundations For Three (book 2)
Montana Fire (book 3)
Montana Promises Box Set (books 1-3)
Hart To Hart (Book 4)

Burning Seduction (Book 5)
Montana Promises Complete Box Set (books 1-5)

ROCK HARD, MONTANA (contemporary romance novellas)
Montana Desire (book 1)
Awakening Passions (book 2)

PLEDGED TO PROTECT (contemporary romantic suspense)
From Panic To Passion (book 1)
From Danger To Desire (book 2)
From Terror To Temptation (book 3)
Pledged To Protect Box Set (books 1-3)

BURIED SERIES (contemporary romantic suspense)
Buried Alive (book 1)
Buried Secrets (book 2)
Buried Deep (book 3)
The Buried Series Complete Box Set (books 1-3)

A NASH MYSTERY (Contemporary Romance)
Sidearms and Silk (book 1)
Black Ops and Lingerie (book 2)
A Nash Mystery Box Set (books 1-2)

STARTER SETS (Romance)
Contemporary
Paranormal

Author Bio

Love it HOT and STEAMY? Sign up for my newsletter and receive MONTANA DESIRE for FREE. smarturl.it/o4cz93?IQid=MLite

OR Are you a fan of quirky PARANORMAL COZY MYSTERIES? Sign up for this newsletter. smarturl.it/CozyNL

Not only do I love to read, write, and dream, I'm an extrovert. I enjoy being around people and am always trying to understand what makes them tick. Not only must my romance books have a happily ever after, I need characters I can relate to. My men are wonderful, dynamic, smart, strong, and the best lovers in the world (of course).

My Paranormal Cozy Mysteries are where I let my imagination run wild with witches and a talking pink iguana who believes he's a real sleuth.

I believe I am the luckiest woman. I do what I love and I have a wonderful, supportive husband, who happens to be hot!

Fun facts about me

(1) I'm a math nerd who loves spreadsheets. Give me numbers and I'll find a pattern.
(2) I live on a Costa Rica beach!
(3) I also like to exercise. Yes, I know I'm odd.

I love hearing from readers either on FB or via email (hint, hint).

Social Media Sites

Website: www.velladay.com
FB: facebook.com/vella.day.90
Twitter: @velladay4
Gmail: velladayauthor@gmail.com